PARADOX

C. DAVID MILLES

For Jo Ann, Bethany, and Owen

Time travel was once considered scientific heresy. I used to avoid talking about it for fear of being labelled a crank. But these days I'm not so cautious.

Stephen Hawking—April 27, 2010

Radio has no future. Heavier-than-air flying machines are impossible. X-rays will prove to be a hoax.

Physicist Lord Kelvin—1899

ONE

"So?"

Zac Ryger didn't notice the voice trying to pierce through his thoughts as he stood at the edge of the pit, envelope in hand. Time seemed to stand still as he stared at the metal cylinder resting next to the pile of dirt. A clean scent hung in the air from the morning rain, and Zac mindlessly nudged some of the wet clumps of dirt with his shoes.

"Zac," the voice interrupted, "are you ready? You're the last one." Zac looked up at his teacher, who smiled and gestured toward the cylinder. "Go ahead."

Zac took a few steps forward and knelt down next to the cylinder. Pretending to shield himself from the wind, he pulled his gray hoodie over his head to hide the tears that were starting to form and carefully put the envelope inside. He took one last look at it, marked with nothing but his name and the year written on it. Blinking hard, he got up and merged with the rest of the students.

"Exciting, isn't it?" Mr. McClane said, adjusting his black beret on his bald head. The air fogged with each word he spoke, and he tucked his hands in the pocket of his leather jacket. "What you're leaving behind today won't ever be seen again for another two hundred years. When you're dead and gone, your body in the ground, you'll still live on through the items you placed in this time capsule." He picked up the silver cylinder and held it up for all to see.

Zac cringed at the mention of death. He hated how people talked about it with such callousness. It was so final, so permanent. So unavoidable. Some people could talk about their dead loved ones without a second thought. Some relived it by witnessing it in their dreams every night.

Mr. McClane sealed the capsule and handed it to the student next to him. "Pass it around," he said. "Hold it in your hands and realize that you are holding history. *Your* history." The students passed it from one to the other, turning it and shaking it to hear its contents. "Even though next year you'll finish high school and get ready to go off to college, two centuries from now your descendants will unearth this." His foot tapped a marker made from marble, engraved with the names of the students whose belongings filled the container. "And it will become their history."

The time capsule made its way to Zac, and he gripped it in his hands, looking down at the metal inscription: *Matheson High School Time Capsule*. He handed it back to the teacher, who dropped it into the pit with a sense of finality. Zac tucked his hands inside his jacket and followed the class back inside the building. He avoided the other students as he made his way back; he didn't want anyone asking him about what he had put in there.

The assignment had been simple. They could put in anything that they wanted to, and they didn't have to tell anyone what it was. It just had to be meaningful to them, and they had to write something about it so that whoever dug it up would have some context for understanding it. Some people put in artifacts from the time period such as a CD they burned of their favorite songs, a book they liked, or some other item they thought would be cool to unearth in the future.

Zac didn't have anything like that. His envelope contained a simple photograph of him and his parents. It was the last picture he had that his mom was in, and it was how he remembered his family. He still had the original at home, but it pained him to put this one in the canister and watch it descend into the ground. It felt like he was burying her all over again.

Maybe now the nightmares would stop. Reliving the moment, seeing the man that took her away from him. In his nightmares, he never saw any details; he just felt the fear and terror. Maybe his dad was going through the same thing. When he found out that Zac was putting something in a time capsule for school, he gave him another sealed envelope in the morning.

"Here," his dad had said. "Do you mind putting this in there, too?"

"What's in it?" Zac asked. He held it up to the light.

"It's for whoever opens it," his dad replied. He gave Zac a stern look. "Promise me you won't open it. Just put it with whatever you have." Zac nodded and folded it in half, putting it inside his own envelope. Maybe someday his dad would tell him what it was.

Now, as they all went back to class, Zac tried to think about what he would say to his dad after school when he asked about the time capsule. And how he'd have to mask his disappointment when his dad would forget his birthday again.

• • •

Zac walked through the doors of his dad's office building. The gleaming white interior of Chronos Labs blinded him, and he had to wait for his eyes to adjust to the lights. The days were getting darker earlier now, something he hated about the winter.

He nodded to the security guard and walked down the hallway, looking at the black and white photographs of mountains and trees.

Rounding the corner, he took a quick breath when he saw her. Emilee was only two years older than he was and had joined Chronos Labs when she graduated from high school.

Zac first met her when his dad was judging the high school science fair about two years ago. He was so impressed with her work that he told her he would give her a job as soon as she graduated, and his company would even pay for her tuition to go to college in town. It was an offer she couldn't pass up.

Zac was also glad she didn't pass it up. "Hi," he said, walking up to the desk.

"Hey, Zac," she said. "Happy birthday."

"Thanks," Zac said. "You mean he didn't forget?"

"No," Emilee said, putting some files in the cabinet. "*He* forgot, but I reminded him." She glanced up, and he was instantly drawn into her brown eyes. She didn't fit the stereotype of a brilliant person like someone would see in the movies. She reminded him of what people would think of as a California surfer girl, with long black hair flowing down to the middle of her back. She wore a bright green headband to hold her hair in place, and freckles dotted her face on the sides of her nose.

Zac extended the cup in his hand. "I got you some coffee," he said. "Caramel Toffee. Your favorite."

"Thanks," she said, taking it. "I could use it right now."

"Rough day?" he asked, trying to make small talk. He always ended up sounding awkward around her. If she noticed, she didn't show it, another reason he liked her. She was nice, but she never really smiled or seemed overly happy. She was always more serious, driven to succeed at whatever she tried her hand at.

"Not really," she said. "Typical day. Classes, lunch... work here... that's about all." She wrote some words down on a piece of paper and taped it above her desk.

"Wow. The wonders of life after high school. Don't you get bored?" Zac asked.

"Sometimes," she said. "But I can't complain. Someday it'll all pan out. I'll look back on this and see that everything happened for a reason. I mean, at least it's a job. And they're paying for my college. I guess I got really lucky."

"Luck?" Zac said. He shook his head. "No way. My dad sometimes talks about you. He says you're going to go places someday. He says it's your destiny."

Emilee smiled. "You're sweet," she said. "Do you believe in destiny like your dad does?"

"Not really," Zac said, pacing around the room. He looked at the framed articles on the wall, reminders of the achievements of his dad's company. Most of them were technical, documenting the physics research pioneered by Chronos Labs. "I just don't like the idea that everything is already planned out for us. I'd like to believe that what I do with my life is up to me." He turned to look at her.

"Me too," she said. She got up and took her jacket off the coat rack near the door, putting it on. "Sorry I gotta leave so fast, but I'm meeting Rock for dinner."

"Oh," Zac said. He fidgeted. "So are... um... you guys going out?"

"Rock? No!" She blushed. "At least... not yet." She paused in the hallway. "But it might turn out that way eventually. I don't know. Right now we're just good friends."

"Yeah," Zac said, trying to sound happy for her. "He's a nice guy. My dad talks about him too. Well, have a nice evening."

She turned and began walking down the hall. "You too. Happy birthday."

Zac watched her leave, then went and sat in her chair, waiting for his dad to come out. He could still smell Emilee's perfume lingering in the air. He knew it was dumb to get his hopes up. She was already out of high school, moving on with her life. She'd be here another few years to finish her degree, and then she'd be gone.

He saw a rubber ball next to the tape dispenser and grabbed it, bouncing it gently on the desk. He hated waiting. It was so quiet with no one else around. He bounced the ball on the floor, seeing how high he could make it go.

What was taking his dad so long? *He probably already forgot I was coming*, Zac thought. *Typical*.

He rose to leave and threw the ball down harder. It hit his foot and rolled away. Zac watched it disappear under a bookcase. Lowering himself, he got down on all fours and reached under it. His fingers felt nothing, and he moved until his eyes were level with the floor. Peering under the bookcase, he saw a faint blue light emanating from it. Allowing his eyes to adjust, he tried to focus on the source of the light but found nothing.

An idea struck him. He got up and turned off the office lights, and immediately, the floor was bathed in a glowing blue light that washed over everything. Zac stood with his face pressed against the wall, trying to see behind the bookcase. The light shone from behind it, too.

He thought he heard a noise and looked over his shoulder. Nothing.

Zac pulled on the bookcase to get a better glimpse behind it and was surprised when it started moving on its own, almost as if there were wheels under it. He stepped back as it opened to reveal a cavity in the wall like a doorway. His hands brushing the wall, he gazed inside.

Behind the bookcase, it looked as if an entirely new hallway stretched as far as he could see. And the source of the blue light had to be at the end of it.

TWO

Eyes trained forward, Zac moved with caution down the new hallway. He felt like Lucy in the *Narnia* books, disappearing deeper where he thought there would have been nothing. Only this wasn't a doorway to a magical land. This passageway was clearly manmade.

His eyes adjusted to the dim light, and he felt the ground dip slightly. The carpet beneath his feet turned into concrete, and he could tell he was walking down an incline. Was the source of the blue light underground? Whatever it was, it reflected off the walls.

Zac stopped, unsure if he should go on. His dad might be waiting for him. And what if the bookcase closed behind him? He could be trapped until someone finds him down here.

He could hear a faint humming sound in the distance beckoning him to continue. He took a deep breath; the air smelled clean down here, almost as if some kind of ultra-air purification system was in place. He pressed forward.

8

Going deeper, the ground seemed to level out, and the blue light grew brighter. The passageway turned a corner, and Zac followed it and immediately saw what was causing the blue light.

In front of him was a large platform, a sort of floor shaped like a pentagon. Surrounding the pentagon on all sides was a cage of glass, looking like its own separate room. Zac couldn't find any door handles; each wall was a solid panel, carefully cut. The pentagon itself looked like it was made of glass or thick plastic, translucent. The light came from something underneath it, though as he approached it, he couldn't tell what it was exactly. It could have been hundreds of light bulbs for all he knew. But as he gazed down through the glass walls, it seemed like source was moving, almost a gel-like substance.

Zac looked around the room for some kind of light switch. There had to be one somewhere. He felt along the walls, trying to distinguish what he could among the shadows. He circled the pentagon and came upon what looked like another hallway. It was dark except for a small bit of light that reflected off a wall in the distance.

How big was this place? Did his dad even know what was down here? He went further down the new hallway toward the other light source. He could hear his footsteps echo off the walls. He stepped as carefully as he could. He had a feeling he shouldn't be down here, but his curiosity tugged at him.

To his left he saw a small office with a computer monitor, the source of the other light. The screensaver swirled, a bright tube-like object moving back and forth across the screen. Zac nudged the mouse with his hand and a new screen popped up.

Three words appeared on the screen: *TEMPUS OPERATOR PASSWORD*. A cursor blinked in the box below it. What did it mean? Whose computer was this? Zac looked around on the desk for a clue,

9

but the desk was bare, cleaned off by its user. Clearly, this person didn't leave anything out for prying eyes.

He looked at the concrete walls around the desk. Being down here reminded him of being in a cave. Once, when he was younger, he and his parents took a tour of a cave and went down inside of it. In the middle of the tour, the lights suddenly went out and blackness engulfed the cave. He thought it was all part of the tour experience, that they just wanted to scare the people and let them see how frightening it was to be lost in a cave. The tour guide turned on his flashlight and insisted that it was not part of the normal tour, then guided them to the exit.

When they reached the exit, they walked into the sunlight only to find trees uprooted, power lines down, and pieces of buildings sprawled out all over the ground. A violent storm had ripped through the area, causing the blackout.

Thinking back to it, Zac was unnerved. What if the lights went out down here? He didn't have a flashlight with him, and he didn't know his way out. He turned to leave, wanting to get back to the office. He'd ask his dad about it when he saw him. Maybe they could come back with flashlights or something.

As he turned to go, something caught the corner of his eye. He saw his reflection in a small piece of glass. He moved closer and saw what looked like a metal box embedded in the concrete wall. It reminded him of the fire extinguisher chambers that were always in buildings, but this one was only the size of a shoe box.

He felt along its edge, searching for some sort of latch. He ran his fingers along the smooth metal and could feel the jagged concrete along its sides. There was nothing.

Zac pressed against the glass, careful not to break it. With a *click*, the small door popped open. He pulled the glass back and peered inside.

All he could see was something that looked like a pen or a small flashlight. He picked it up, turning it over in his fingers. It didn't look like anything extraordinary. Probably just a small flashlight for emergencies. He squinted in the darkness and put it close to his eyes, trying to figure out how to turn it on. The light was too dim; he'd have to take it someplace brighter.

Finding his bearings, he made his way back to the room with the blue pentagon. By now he had lost track of time. He'd have to just get a quick glance at the object and rush back up to his dad's office. For once, he was actually grateful that his dad seemed to have forgotten about him for a little while.

As Zac approached the source of the light, he nearly jumped when he heard a hissing sound. One of the glass panels around the pentagon swung open, and the humming sound grew louder.

Zac looked around the room, searching for someone else who might have walked in and remotely opened the door.

No one was there. With trepidation, he stepped into the glass enclosure and looked down at the blue lights. They swirled, thick strands of a darker shade joining each other and expanding, then sinking down into the substance. It reminded him of a lava lamp.

Zac held the object in front of him and searched for something that might show him how to turn it on. It was the size of a magic marker and was made from a lightweight metal. It was different than any other flashlight he'd seen before. The casing was textured and had a thin strip on the side of it that reflected the light and looked like an LED screen.

The top of the device was made of the same kind of material. It was round and flat. Zac held it to his eye, and it looked like he was looking back at himself. He could make out something deep inside the object, something that looked like a computer chip.

The humming grew louder as he paced back and forth on the pentagon. He could feel heat coming from the floor and was filled with a sense of unease. At that moment, he had the strange desire to call out to someone, to not be alone.

He gave the pen-like object one more glance. Why was there a computer chip inside it? He gripped it in his hand and placed his thumb on the smooth surface on the top of the object.

In an instant, Zac felt his body surge with a violent heave. Blue light exploded all around him, and the air was filled with a buzzing sound like a machine vibrating violently. His body shook, and he felt a numbing sensation as his ears started ringing.

He could feel something like electricity in the fillings of his teeth. He struggled to breathe. It was like someone had hit him in the chest, knocking the wind out of him. His heart pounded like a hammer smashing against his rib cage, threatening to jump out.

What was probably only seconds felt like an eternity as he tried in vain to move out of the pentagon. His knees began to give, and he collapsed to the floor, his legs shaking like jelly. The blue light faded, and he his ears soon filled with sound. Air rushed into his lungs, and he gasped for breath, clutching his chest as his heart struggled to regain its rhythm.

Sensation flowed back into his hands, and he could feel something soft under them. Something smooth. His vision was still blurred, although it was coming back into focus. He felt queasy, his stomach lurching. Without warning, he vomited, the acidic taste lingering in his mouth. He coughed and his throat burned.

Zac remained still for a few moments, collecting himself. As everything came back into focus, he stood up and looked around. Something wasn't right.

The glowing blue pentagon was nowhere in sight. The concrete walls, the underground hallway… everything was gone.

Instead of solid floor below his feet, he saw grass, some of it covered with splotches of his vomit.

He looked behind him and saw what looked like the city. It seemed to him like he was in a park or a field. What had happened? Did he just dream everything earlier? Or black out on the way to his dad's office?

He ran toward the lights of the city, searching for the office building. It was missing. But that was impossible. He recognized all of the other buildings around him. But his dad's building was missing. *How could it be missing?* Zac thought. *It's been there for ten years.*

It was dark outside, much darker than when he had arrived at the office. But now, the sun was just below the horizon in the east. By the look of the sky, it must've been early morning rather than dinner time. Strange.

Zac pulled out his cell phone. The display was blank. His battery must have died. He knew he had to find a way to get ahold of his dad. He saw the hospital across the street and knew that someone would be there no matter what time it was. He started to go when his foot hit something. He bent down to pick it up.

In his hand, he held the small cylindrical device that he found behind the glass. Only now, the thin reflective strip down the side was illuminated with several glowing bars.

THREE

The hospital was buzzing with activity when Zac walked through the doors. The morning sun was just rising over the horizon outside, casting a pale yellow light over the streets and buildings. The blinding glare reflected off the glass windows, and he shielded his eyes to block the sun.

He looked for a phone that he could use. A man moved past him in a hurry, pushing a wheelchair. Zac spun around and watched, standing in the middle of the hallway.

"Can I help you, sir?" a voice behind him said.

Zac turned to see a woman with black, shoulder-length hair. She wore a polo shirt with the hospital's name embroidered on it and carried a clipboard in her left hand.

"Oh, sorry," he said, looking around the hospital as he answered. Something about this place seemed different, he thought. He hadn't actually been in the hospital for a while, but it just looked...

"Can I help you find someone?" the woman asked, interrupting his thoughts. She walked backward, leading him to a desk with a computer. She set her clipboard down and began typing something. The keyboard was outdated, and the monitor was large and bulky. It looked like the hospital hadn't upgraded their computers for a long time.

Zac tried clearing his thoughts, taking his attention off his surroundings. "Sorry," he said, "I'm not here to visit a patient. I just need to use a phone to call my dad."

"Your dad?"

"Yeah. His name's Daniel Ryger. If I can just use a phone…"

"Hold on, please," she said. She typed at the keyboard and stared at the screen, waiting. "Okay, it says we have a Ryger registered on the eighth floor in Maternity."

"Huh?" Zac said. "No, he's not a patient; I just need to call him."

The woman stood back, cocking her head in confusion. "So wait," she said, holding her hands up, "I'm a bit unclear as to what you're asking me for. Are you a family member or a friend?"

Zac shifted with uneasiness. He felt like he was being interrogated. Maybe if he could just slip past her, he could find someone else who didn't seem to be in a hurry and who would actually listen.

"Yeah," Zac said, trying his best not to sound like he was lying, "I'm family. Thanks for your help." He smiled, hoping she wouldn't see through him as he walked down the hallway toward the elevator. He quickened his pace, casting a glance over his shoulder. The woman was still watching him. He slowed his walk so he wouldn't seem suspicious.

Passing a drinking fountain, he stopped to get a drink, trying to wash away the bitter taste of vomit from earlier. Seeing the elevator ahead, he moved on, eager to get out of the woman's line of sight.

He pressed the button and waited. The elevator seemed to be taking forever. Maybe he should take the stairs. But if the woman thought he was acting strange earlier, ducking into a stairwell might not seem like the best idea.

The light above the elevator slowly made its way to the button for the ground level. Nervous, Zac put his hands in his pocket and felt the pen-like device. He pulled it out and looked at it. It definitely wasn't a flashlight. This was the brightest light he'd seen it in so far, but it didn't seem to help much. He couldn't tell what it was. The lights on the side of the object were still there, though he had no clue why it was lighting up now. Something happened back in that strange room that made it turn on. But it didn't make any sense that he would suddenly go from being inside that room to being outside.

Unless…

Deep in the back of his mind, Zac had a thought. Maybe this was some sort of a prank. Someone had followed him and wanted to mess with his mind. Someone had found him in that room and had done something to him and left him outside. And now that he was recovering, nothing seemed right. It would explain why he started vomiting and feeling dizzy. It was the effects of whatever they used on him.

The elevator doors opened, and Zac stepped inside. He stared at the row of buttons, not sure what one to press or where he should go. The door was sliding closed when a hand shot through the opening and the doors retracted.

"Sorry," said the man who stepped in. He carried a briefcase and was wearing a long, tan overcoat that reached down to his ankles. His glasses framed his face under the rim of his dark brown hat, and Zac could see beads of sweat trickling down the sides of his nose, collecting at his mustache. "What a day. Not going to make it to work on time today, but it's for a good reason."

Zac smiled but stared ahead. He hated elevators. It was always awkward being trapped in the small space with people he didn't know, forced to make small talk or to maintain an awkward silence. "What floor?" he asked.

"Eighth," the man said.

Zac pressed the button. The elevator lurched, and he could feel the pull of gravity as it traveled up to the higher floors.

"You going to eight, too?" the man asked when Zac didn't press another button.

"Me?" Zac said, caught off guard. He stared straight ahead, determined not to make eye contact. "No. I mean, for a moment. I just need to find somebody."

The man nodded, and then added, "He's my first. My wife's totally calm about it, but I'm a nervous wreck."

"About what?" Zac asked, not sure what the man was talking about. He could see the man's blurry reflection in the metal elevator door, but he couldn't bring himself to turn and talk to him.

"Being a father for the first time," the man said, wiping his brow with his coat sleeve. "I have no idea what to do with kids. But everyone says you can't prepare to be a parent, it just sort of 'kicks in,' and you get this whole parental instinct that takes over." He gave a nervous laugh.

"I'm sure you'll be a great dad," Zac said, watching the light climb through the row of numbers, moving from six to seven.

"I sure hope so. I haven't been able to stop worrying. We only picked out the name last night. Isaac. My wife's not too crazy about the name, but we compromised. She'll probably call the little guy 'Zac' for short." The man smiled at the sound of it. "Isaac Joshua Ryger. I think it has a nice ring to it."

The elevator stopped, and the door opened. The man stepped out, but Zac stood, not moving. "Wait a minute," he said. "What's his name?"

"Isaac."

Zac took a step out of the elevator. "Did you say your last name's Ryger?"

"Yes," the man replied. He held out his hand for Zac to shake. "Daniel Ryger. And you are?"

Zac took his hand and looked with stunned curiosity at the man. Now that he was actually looking at him, he saw an obvious resemblance. But there was no way... the man facing him looked just like pictures Zac had seen of his dad from years ago. But Zac never remembered him having a mustache.

"Dad..." Zac said in a whisper.

"I'm sorry," Daniel Ryger said, "I didn't catch that. Did you say your name is Dan?"

"You're... you're my..." Zac stopped short. "But you're younger..."

The man pulled his hand free and gave an uneasy smile. "Well, I hate to be rude, but I need to go see my new son. He's right down the hall." He hurried down the hallway toward the glass windows, taking off his hat and stopping to stare at what was behind it.

Zac stood at the end of the hallway, watching the man. This man who had the same name as his own dad. This man who had a son with the same name as his own.

Zac walked toward the man and when he was closer, turned to see the baby the man was looking at through the window.

"Is... is that him?" Zac asked.

"Yep. That's him," the man beamed. "Isn't he beautiful? The whole world awaits him. I can't help wondering what he'll do with his life. All the possibilities… and who knows what the future holds for him?"

Zac stared at the baby, bundled tightly and laying in the plastic crib, sleeping soundly. "What's today's date?" he asked without taking his eyes off the newborn.

"September 22," the man answered. "A date I'll never forget. Today's the day when my whole life changed for the better."

As Zac looked on, watching the tiny little person in front of him start to squirm, trying to get his arm out of the swaddling, a sudden realization came to him. He didn't know why, but if what he thought was correct, then this man standing next to him was his father.

And the baby in front of him opening its eyes, blinking in the light… that baby was *him*.

FOUR

Zac stood entranced, staring at the baby that was supposedly him. It didn't make sense. It had to be a dream.

He watched as the nurse came to the window and grabbed the cart, rolling the baby away and putting it back with the others. The baby cried, and she smiled at it, gently touching its feet and saying something Zac couldn't hear.

"Sir?" came a voice from behind him. Zac turned to see a man, another nurse in the maternity ward. He was pushing another wooden cart with a baby in a plastic crib on top, taking it back to the nursery. "Sorry. I just need to squeeze by."

"Sure," Zac said, backing up. He turned to watch the nurse and realized the man that he was talking to, the one who said his name was Daniel Ryger, was gone. "Hey," he called to the nurse, "did you see where that man went?"

"I'm sorry?"

"There was a man standing right next to me," he said, pointing down the hallway, "and I needed to ask him a question. Can you tell me where he went?"

"Are you family?" the man asked. He paused and nodded to another nurse through the glass. She opened the large door and took the baby in with her.

"No," Zac said. "Well, sort of. I mean…"

"Well, if you're not family, I'm afraid you can't go back to patient rooms during these hours," he said. "Visiting hours are between ten and ten. You can come back in a few hours if you want."

Zac shook his head. "I need to talk to him *now*," he said. "It will just take a minute." He started to move, but the nurse held out his hands to block the way.

"I'm sorry," he said, "but we need to respect our patients' privacy, and believe me, these new moms need all the sleep they can get right now. You'll have to come back later."

Zac sighed. "Okay," he said. "Thanks anyway." He turned and walked back to the elevator. Stepping inside, he pressed the button and waited to arrive at the ground floor.

He had a thought. He could just wait down in the lobby, sit in a chair and pretend to read a magazine or something. If the man he talked to was his dad, he had to come back down sometime, and then Zac could confront him and try to figure out what was happening.

He found a comfortable chair near the lobby windows, close to the entrance. Now he could watch the door, too. From this place, he could see anyone who left the hospital. His eyes started to blur, and a heaviness fell over him. His eyes began to close, but he tried to shake off the sleepiness.

No, he told himself. He had to stay awake. Then again, if he shut his eyes for just a few minutes, it wouldn't hurt. Maybe he'd

21

wake up and find this was all some ridiculous dream. His eyes slowly closed, and he drifted off.

A loud crash jolted Zac awake, and he nearly fell out of his chair. He looked around, confused at his surroundings, and then remembered that he was at the hospital. People were rushing past him to see something outside, and he turned to see.

The sun was fully up now, its light pouring into the lobby. He walked over to the entrance and saw what everyone was looking at.

Across the street, two cars had collided. A small silver one was smashed against the side of a brick building. It looked like the white pickup truck had hit the other, pushing it into the wall. Zac could see people in the vehicles, but no one was helping. Everyone was just staring in shock like people who slow down just to look at an accident on the side of the road. Wasn't anybody going to help them?

Zac took a step forward. They were right in front of the hospital, so someone would be out in a minute. But if no one was going to run over and see if they needed help, he would. He started across the street.

As he stepped off the curb, a hand grabbed his shoulder. A tall male with short blond hair who was wearing all black pulled him back with an iron grip. "Let it go," he said.

Zac shrugged him off and wrenched his shoulder free. He kept walking. The stranger raced around him and held his hands in front of him, trying to hold Zac back. His hat was pulled low, the brim hiding his eyes. "You need to come with me."

"Let go of me, man!" Zac shouted, and darted to his right. "Someone has to do something. Instead of pushing me back, why don't you come help me?"

He stayed behind as Zac approached the vehicles. A man in a plaid shirt and blue jeans got out of the pickup truck, dazed, but able to stand. He was groaning and holding his rib cage.

"You okay?" Zac asked. The man nodded and walked toward the crowd. Zac moved to the silver car and looked inside. A man in a business suit was slumped over the steering wheel, his arm extended around his head and touching the dashboard. Zac turned to the crowd of onlookers. "Can anybody help me get him out? He's not moving!" Finally, three paramedics rushed out of the hospital wheeling a stretcher.

"Stand aside, please," they said. "We can take it from here." They opened the door and lifted the man onto the stretcher, strapping him down. The crowd parted as the paramedics made their way to the doors.

Whispers filled the air. "Is that the mayor?" someone asked.

Zac watched the doors close behind the paramedics and felt a tap on his shoulder. He turned to see the same guy who had restrained him earlier.

"That was not a very bright thing you did," he said. He looked to be about four or five years older than Zac.

"It was more than *you* did," Zac said, taking offense.

The stranger looked around him, paranoid. "Come on," he said. "We have to get out of here right now. This wasn't supposed to happen. Someone could see you."

"What are you talking about? All of these people see me!"

"Exactly," he replied. He began leading Zac away from the crowd. "I need you to come with me."

"I'm not going anywhere with you!" Zac said, his voice rising. "I don't even know who you are."

"I'm Bryce," he said. A van pulled up and someone with a video camera got out. The side of the van was emblazoned with the words *News 2* in bright red and blue. "Crap. Okay," Bryce said, turning to face Zac. "You have two choices. Either you can follow me now, or I'll *make* you follow me. But it won't be pleasant."

"*Make* me?" Bryce was a few inches taller than Zac, but he didn't let that intimidate him. He'd dealt with people like this guy enough before to know not to back down.

They heard someone yelling from the site of the crash. "There he is," they said. "Over there." A man in a button-up shirt and a necktie walked over with a camera and started taking pictures of Zac and Bryce.

"Oh, great," Bryce said, covering his face, "this is *not* happening. Not now."

The group started asking Zac questions about the ordeal and what he saw, if he had talked to the mayor, and a bunch of others he couldn't make out.

Bryce leaned in and whispered into his ear with urgency. "Ignore these people. Just follow me. I'm going to take you to your dad."

"My dad?" That grabbed Zac's attention. "Where is he?" But Bryce was already walking, moving away from the hospital. "Wait a minute," he called, following and trying to keep up. "My dad's back *there*. We're going the wrong way."

Bryce led him into an alley. He looked around the corner, searching. After a few moments, he turned back to Zac.

"Okay," he said, almost out of breath. "You still have that thing that looks like a flashlight on you?"

Zac dug into his pockets. "You mean this?" he said, holding it up. "How'd you know about it?"

Bryce breathed a sigh of relief as he rolled his eyes. "Thank God. It's still lit up. Okay, if you want to see your dad, you have to do exactly what I say." He adjusted the thin black tube in Zac's palm and closed his hand around it, making a fist. "I'm going to count to three. When I do, hold on to that as tightly as you can and then press your thumb onto the top, very firmly. Think you can do that?"

"Yeah," Zac said, nodding. "But what does—"

"No time for questions," Bryce said. He took a deep breath and held out a similar object to the one Zac held in his hand. He raised his thumb above it, too. "I hope to God this works," he said, looking Zac in the eyes.

"Hope what works?"

"One... two... *three!*"

Zac pressed his thumb down, and suddenly the world around him swirled into a mass of colors, blurring everything in sight. His body trembled and his arms felt a jolt surge through them, causing his whole body to tingle like when his foot fell asleep. A high-pitched whirring noise pierced his ears, and everything around him turned black.

With a violent lurch, he felt his feet strike something hard and his ears popped. His head pounded, and his eyes were filled with a bright light. He squinted to shut it out.

He felt dizzy, and his legs felt like spaghetti. He stumbled backward, losing his balance and fell onto his back. His breathing was labored, and he could hear his heart thumping as it pumped blood through his body. His hearing came back, and he strained to open his eyes, taking in the bright blue light. The air seemed different. He heard a voice behind him.

"Thank you, Bryce," the voice said. Zac moved his jaw some more, and his ears popped again. He could hear more clearly. "I have no idea how all this happened, but I am forever in your debt."

"Not a problem, Dr. Ryger. He's back. But now that he knows, I guess the question now is whether or not we should train him."

FIVE

Zac turned to see his dad talking to Bryce, bathed in the shimmering blue light. He looked down to see that he was sitting on the pentagon that he had seen just a few hours earlier. Was everything that had just happened all in his mind? Had he simply passed out?

His dad knelt in front of him, shining a flashlight in his eyes. "Okay, this is going to sound stupid, but can you tell me what your name is?"

Zac squinted as he looked into the light. "Yeah, Dad. It's Zac. Why are you asking me—"

"And what is your birth date?" he asked, moving the light back and forth, watching Zac's eyes follow it.

"September 22. Why are you asking me that?"

His dad sighed. "Sorry, Zac, but you hit your head pretty hard and were passed out when we found you. Okay, one more question. What year is it now?"

Zac pushed the flashlight away and stood up. "This is stupid. I'm not going to answer obvious questions." He stepped out of the pentagon and looked around, surveying the concrete room. "This is all under your building. How did you know I was down here?"

Dr. Ryger sighed. "I saw that the bookcase was moved, so I looked behind it. I had a feeling you followed the hallway down."

"You didn't know this was all down here?" Zac asked.

His dad was silent, and he exchanged glances with Bryce. "No."

Bryce spoke. "Your dad was worried when he couldn't find you," he said. "We searched for you, and we finally found you down here. You must have slipped. You were passed out in the middle of the floor, and I was able to help you regain consciousness."

"I don't understand," Zac said. "My dream was so vivid."

"Your brain was probably just trying to make sense of the voices you heard while you were unconscious," Bryce said. "That happens with dreams a lot."

His dad came over and took him by the arm. "We need to get home, Zac. I want you to just get some rest. You'll be fine in the morning."

Zac took one last look at the room and followed his dad up the concrete walkway toward the office. They exited through the space behind the bookcase and Bryce nudged it. The bookcase slid back into place.

"What are those rooms?" Zac asked.

"I don't have a clue," Dr. Ryger replied. "I'll talk to someone about them in the morning. Just go wait in the car for a second, okay? I need to talk to Bryce for a minute."

Zac started down the hallway but stopped to listen. He pressed himself against the wall and strained to make out their hushed tones.

"He's going to start asking questions," Bryce said, a hint of urgency in his voice.

His dad's voice was calmer. "It'll all be taken care of. We've already fed him what he needs to know to make sense of the experience. You heard him—it was just a vivid dream. He hit his head."

"But it's more than that! I told you, he was seen!"

"Well..." his dad trailed off. "How bad was it? Was it significant?"

"There were cameras," Bryce said. "He acted. He could have changed things."

A long silence hung in the air. Zac stepped back toward the entrance, afraid they might find him listening. They could come around the corner at any moment. Finally, his dad spoke.

"I doubt it," he said. "We would know by now."

"Would we?" Bryce asked. "Maybe the changes haven't reached us yet. We need to talk to him, find out what he did."

"That's out of the question," his dad said. "He can't know."

"He already *does* know. He's going to start asking about what he saw downstairs."

"Emilee shouldn't have left Zac in the room alone."

"Regardless, you need to question him. We need to know how he got the Wand to work. Those things only work for *one* person. And one's never been programmed for him."

Zac's dad sighed. "I know," he said. "I have a lot to figure out tonight when I get home. But I'm not ready to start talking about it with him. You know the first thing he'd want to do if he figured out what we're doing down there."

"Yeah," Bryce said. "You'd better go. He's been out there for a while, and he'll be wondering what's taking you so long. If you want to keep this secret from him, you'd better get going."

Zac could hear footsteps start down the hallway and sprinted for the door, hurling himself outside. He raced to the car and got in, trying to catch his breath as he saw his dad exit the building's lobby doors. He pretended to be dozing off as he heard the car door open. He acted like he was startled awake.

"Sorry," Dr. Ryger said, sitting down and buckling up. "Business. I told Bryce that we need to sort through a few details."

Zac yawned. He still felt nauseous from the experience earlier. "Sorry I worried you," he said. "You seriously didn't know about those rooms down there?"

His dad shook his head as he started the car and backed up. "Never saw them before. Probably some kind of control room for regulating the building's conditions. We have to monitor lots of different variables for the work we do here. I'll talk to someone tomorrow to see what I can find out. They really need to tell us these things."

Zac didn't say much to his dad after they got home. He knew he didn't just pass out and hit his head. He didn't just dream of seeing his dad years ago. Something else had happened. And his dad knew something about it.

He lay awake in his bed, wondering how he could find out. Did Emilee know? She didn't seem to. Like his dad and Bryce had said earlier, she left him alone, probably because she didn't know there was something they were trying to protect. There had to be another way. Maybe there was something in the house, some paperwork in a briefcase somewhere.

Zac opened his bedroom door and looked down the hallway. The house was dark except for the light they kept on at night in the living room. He moved across the carpeted floor, taking care not to step in the places where the floor creaked. If he couldn't find anything himself, he'd have to ask his dad. But even Zac knew that would just result in more lies, more cover-up.

He came to the end of the hallway and heard movement in the lighted room. His dad was still awake.

"...gotta be in here somewhere..." his dad said, talking to himself. "I'd remember seeing something like that."

Zac approached unnoticed. His dad was sitting in a chair, a brown box with a white label resting on top of the table. Papers were scattered everywhere.

Zac's dad was leafing through a newspaper, one that looked yellowed with age. He came to a page and suddenly stopped. Zac watched as his dad propped his elbows on the table, putting his head in his hands.

"No..." he whispered, fingers pushing through his hair. He pushed the newspaper away and sank back into his chair.

Zac entered the room, speaking quietly so he wouldn't startle his dad. "Hey," he said. His dad jumped. "I couldn't sleep."

"Me neither," Dr. Ryger said. He closed the paper and tossed it back in the box. "Just going through some stuff."

"What stuff?" Zac asked, craning his neck to get a better look.

"Oh, nothing much." He put his hand on the box, tapping it. "I was looking for some of your medical records." He hesitated. "Just in case we... um... needed them because of the injury you... uh... had when you hit your head..."

You're lying, Zac thought. *You always stammer when you're not telling the truth.* "What were you reading?" he asked.

"Oh, *that?*" he asked, looking at the paper. "I just found an old paper from when you were born. I got sidetracked and started looking at it, reminiscing... it's just kind of neat to look back, I guess." He looked at the clock. "Wow; I didn't realize it was this late. I'm going to turn in for the night. Hey, sorry we forgot to celebrate your birthday. We can do it tomorrow. Turn off the light on your way out, would you please?" He walked past Zac, not making eye contact.

Zac waited until it was clear, then went over to the newspaper, opening it up. It was actually a paper from September 23. His dad had told him a while back that he bought the one from the day *after* Zac was born because all of these stories were about events that happened *on* the day he was born.

He flipped through it, examining the headlines, scanning them for information. He turned the page and a picture in the bottom-right corner caught his eye. It was the same car and pick-up truck he had seen during his experience. The headline in the accompanying article read: "Mayor Injured in Car Crash."

Weird, he thought, vaguely recalling someone pointing out the mayor on the stretcher, right before Bryce appeared. He studied the picture, remembering every vivid detail. Everything was the same, from the vehicles in the crash to the brick building the car slammed into. Even the puddles of fluid spilled out from the vehicles onto the ground in the same way.

His attention was caught by a person in the corner of the photo. *It can't be*, he told himself. He held the picture closer, focusing on the face of the individual. Immediately he knew who it was that he was looking at in the picture; there could be no doubt who it was walking toward the vehicles at the crash site.

He was staring at a picture of himself.

SIX

Zac looked away from the old newspaper, thinking that his eyes must be playing tricks on him. How could he be in a newspaper from the day after he was born? That couldn't be him in the picture. Could it?

He had a million questions that he wanted to ask his dad, but he knew that it would be pointless. His dad would just deny everything, would just try to convince him that it had all been in his head. He had to catch him off guard. Zac knew that as long as it was just his word against his dad's story, there was no chance of getting the answers he wanted. He had to ask him when there were other people around, when he might slip up. His dad might be able to lie to *him*, but to try to convince several people at the same time... well, that would be a bit tougher.

Zac took the newspaper to his bedroom. It was late now. He'd have to wait until morning. When his dad thought he was at school, *that's* when he'd carry out his plan. He'd surprise him at

32

work, and then he would see how long his dad could keep up this charade.

The morning couldn't come fast enough for Zac. He stayed in bed, listening to his dad get ready for work. His dad rarely checked in with him before school. Today wasn't any different.

Zac heard the door close and the garage open, followed by the running of the car's engine. He got out of bed and got dressed, anxious to leave the house. He knew he couldn't leave too soon, though. It had to be in the middle of the day, a time when his dad wouldn't expect him.

He waited until about ten in the morning, then drove to his dad's office building. He entered the doors and was stopped by the security guard.

"Hello," he said. "Here to see your dad?"

"Yeah," Zac said. "Just stopping by."

"Aren't you supposed to be in school right now?"

Zac had to think quickly. "I got a pass to leave for lunch."

"Oh," the security guard replied. "I see. You want me to buzz him, let him know you're here?"

"No," Zac said. "It's supposed to be a surprise. I'm going to take him out for lunch in a bit."

The security guard nodded. "Sounds good. Go on back." He smiled and wrote something down, then turned back to his work.

Zac made his way down the hallway and found Emilee sitting at the desk in the front. A look of confusion crossed her face when she saw Zac.

"Zac? What are you doing here?"

"Just stopping by," he said. "Do you know where my dad is? I need to see him."

"He's..." Emilee said, then stopped herself. She hesitated for a moment. "He's in a meeting right now. I can just give him the message if you tell me what it is." She offered a smile.

Zac turned and started down the hallway. "That's okay," he said. "I'll go wait outside his door. It'll only be a minute." He moved through the bright corridor, heading toward the conference room door. He'd only been in the room a few times before. It was large and had a long, wooden table in the middle of it, chairs surrounding it on all sides. He wasn't planning on waiting, though. He was just going to stroll in and interrupt. It would make his dad mad at first, but then he would pull Zac aside to talk. He'd know that Zac meant business, and he wasn't leaving until he got answers.

Emilee hurried after him, trying to get him to wait in the lobby. "You can't go back there," she said. "He's in a meeting with investors!"

Zac pretended not to hear her. He approached the door and pulled down on the metal handle, not bothering to knock.

"Wait!" he heard Emilee say. But it was too late.

Sitting around the table were about ten men in business suits. They looked up when Zac entered, and his dad stopped speaking. A look of surprise registered on his face.

"Zac? What are you doing here?"

Zac walked next to the spot where his dad was sitting and took off his backpack. From it, he pulled the newspaper and tossed it onto the table in front of his dad. It was folded back to display the picture with Zac in it.

"Care to tell me why you were looking at this last night?" he asked.

Dr. Ryger looked up at him, then shot a quick glance at Emilee.

"I'm so sorry, Dr. Ryger," she said, almost pleading for forgiveness. "He just walked past me and went straight toward the room. I didn't know what he was doing."

For a split second, Zac felt sorry for her. He might have gotten her in trouble. Hopefully she wouldn't lose her job or anything. No, his dad would never fire her. Not for something like this, even though his eyes said something different.

"Daniel," said one of the investors, "what's all this about?"

Zac's dad abruptly changed demeanor, turning on his businessman-like charm. "I assure you, gentlemen, it's nothing." He gave a broad smile. "I apologize for my son's rudeness, and I hope that this does not reflect poorly on your decision to fund the research." He looked at his watch. "But perhaps today we should cut this meeting short. I will be happy to meet with you all again next week if you'd like. Just leave your information with Emilee and she'll call you to set up an appointment."

The men got up to leave, some looking perplexed, some irritated. Dr. Ryger shook their hands as they passed, and they handed their business cards to Emilee. When they had gone, he turned to her. "Shut the door, please," he said.

Zac had a sudden feeling of uneasiness, but he stood his ground.

"What's this all about, Zac?" he said, sitting down. He brushed his hand against the newspaper as if dismissing it. "Why'd you bring this here in the middle of the day, interrupting a meeting with important people? Do you have any idea how much money you might have cost me?"

"I want you to explain this," he said pointing to the picture and sitting next to him.

His dad leaned closer in to him, ignoring the picture completely, shoving the newspaper aside. Emilee walked over and picked it up.

"And your questions couldn't wait?" he asked. "Do you realize that those men are responsible for funding my research here?" He threw up his hands and leaned back in his chair. "Because without them, Zac, my work isn't possible. If I don't have their money, I don't have a job. And if I don't have a job, we don't have a house."

Zac shook his head. "Don't try to avoid the question. Why were you so intent on staring at that picture last night, Dad?" Dr. Ryger was silent. "I *saw* you!" Zac said.

Emilee looked at it, stunned. She sat down across from Dr. Ryger. "Is this…"

Dr. Ryger held up his hand to silence her. "I think we need to get you to a doctor, Zac."

Zac reached across the table and grabbed the newspaper from Emilee. "Why am I in that picture?" he asked, pointing to himself on the worn paper. "And don't say you don't know, because we both know you're hiding something." Zac pushed the paper in front of him. "I heard you and Bryce talking last night."

His dad sighed, resting his elbows on the table. He put his hand to his face, exhausted from the conversation. "What you think you heard—"

"What I *did* hear," Zac interrupted. "I heard the way you were talking about me. I knew something was up. And then I see *this*," he said, gesturing toward the photo. "What happened to me last night? What was that room downstairs?"

"I don't know," his dad said, not missing a beat.

Zac could see it in his eyes; he was lying.

"Then what were you two talking about?" he asked. He smiled and turned to Emilee. "Did you know there's a secret room behind the bookcase near your desk?"

She looked down at her lap as if hiding something. Her hands fidgeted.

"I haven't told her about it yet," his dad said. "I was going to——"

"Yes," Emilee said. "Yes, I knew."

A stunned silence hung in the room. After a few moments, Zac's dad spoke.

"You signed a sworn affidavit, Emilee."

"He clearly knows something," she said. She looked up. "How long can you keep this up? I think we just need to tell him. He's not some random person. He's your son."

"We?" Zac said. "You mean... you knew about that room, too? You knew what's down there?"

"Zac," his dad said, "there are some things that are just better left unknown."

"But I *want* to know," Zac said. "That's *me* in that old picture; I know it is! Just please, tell me what you know. Anything. I just want to know what happened to me last night. I won't let up until you at least tell me what you know."

His dad and Emilee exchanged glances. "You'd better go get Bryce," he said. "I may need his help explaining things." He stared intently at Zac. "Son, if I told you what I know, you'd call me a liar anyway. You wouldn't believe me."

"Try me," Zac said. "I want to believe."

Dr. Ryger sighed. He pushed the newspaper in front of Zac. "Okay," he said. "But you have to understand that what I say never leaves this room."

Zac nodded.

"Yes, that is you in the newspaper."

Zac's eyes widened. "I knew it," he said. "But how? Is it digitally edited or something?"

"No," Dr. Ryger said. "Here's where it's going to sound like I'm lying to you. When you stepped inside that blue pentagon, you travelled through time. And the scary thing is, we have no idea how you did it. It should have been impossible."

SEVEN

"Time travel? Why won't you tell me the truth?" Zac asked, indignant. He kicked back in his chair. "I'm not stupid. Time travel is impossible. I want the real truth."

"That *is* the real truth, Zac. It's what I do here."

"What do you mean?"

"What do you know about my research?" his dad asked. "How much do you really know about my job? Have you ever seen me bring anything home from work?"

Zac thought about it. "No," he said finally.

"Of course not," he said. "There's a reason for that."

"But I thought you just did research in the field of physics," Zac said. "Isn't that what this place is?" He looked around the room, which seemed like a perfectly generic conference room.

"No," Dr. Ryger said. "It's just a cover for what I really do. And now I have to inform the proper authorities that you know, too." He sighed. "They aren't going to be happy, but I'll have to explain everything to them."

"But that doesn't make sense," Zac said. "Time travel? That's only in the movies."

"I know it sounds bizarre..."

Zac got out of his chair and walked over to the window and leaned against it. "Dad, are you hearing yourself? You're sitting there telling me that people can travel through time, and that I just did it accidentally. And it's been this huge big secret all along, and... and..." He shook his head, unable to take it all in. "Do you realize how insane you sound?"

"Zac, look, I—"

"Okay, here's a question for you. If time travel is really possible, then where are all the visitors from the future? Why aren't we seeing people from the future coming here telling us not to do some of the stupid things we do like start wars and... and..." His frustration began to show as he talked faster, motioning with his hands. He began pacing the room. "If time travel is really happening, then why aren't our future selves coming to tell us what to do, like to avoid big mistakes?"

"I don't think you understand," his dad said, trying to stay calm. "It doesn't work like that. There are certain rules."

"No, *you* don't understand," Zac said, voice rising. His dad's eyes darted to the door, and he motioned with his hand for Zac to lower his voice. "I think you're full of it. I think you're just trying to feed me some more science fiction bull like those stories you used to tell me when I was little." He jabbed his finger in the air at his dad. "I'm not a kid anymore, and I'm not going to be played with. There's no such thing as time travel!"

The door opened. "Actually, there is," said Bryce, stepping in. Emilee was at his side, and she shut the door behind them. Bryce gestured for Zac to take a seat again while he sat down. "So Emilee says you're now in the loop about our little research experiment going on here, huh?"

Zac sat down but refused to look at anyone. This was ridiculous. All he wanted was for someone to level with him, to give him a straight answer.

Dr. Ryger turned to Bryce. "I don't think he's going to buy it, hearing it from me. How about you try explaining it to him? He thinks I'm lying to him."

"Because you *are*," Zac said. And now two other people were too. Even though they weren't friends, he thought Emilee would at least do him the courtesy of not playing into this.

"I'll tell you what," Bryce said. "Let me ask you to assume for the moment that time travel is possible. Can you do that?"

Zac sneered. "What are you? My dad's boss?"

"No," Bryce said, "I'm one of his assistants. Emilee is, too. Your dad hired me when I started college. But just assume for a minute that time travel is possible. Then maybe the rest of what I say will make sense to you."

"I can't just do that," Zac said. "You're asking me to believe something ludicrous."

Bryce shrugged. "Don't you do that all the time when you watch a movie? You allow yourself to believe that aliens can invade, or that teenagers can get super powers from being bitten by a spider."

Zac was silent. He looked over at Emilee, who met his gaze. She remained serious, focused on Bryce. Emilee was smart. If she seemed to be listening to his dad and Bryce, then maybe there was a ring of truth to it. He could at least hear them out.

"Fine," he said, rolling his eyes. "Let's assume that time travel is possible. What does that have to do with this place?"

"This," Bryce said, taking over the conversation, "is where we house the project. You saw it last night when you went down that corridor. Ordinarily, our security wouldn't let someone get that far, but being Dr. Ryger's son, you were allowed in the building. That, and we're not exactly connected to the government."

"Wait a minute. How can you have some big, top-secret project going on under an office building like this? You're telling me no one knows that it's down there?"

Dr. Ryger broke in. "It's not actually that hard to believe. When Oppenheimer was working on the atom bomb with the Manhattan Project, it was all being done under a college, and the college president didn't even know about it."

"True," said Bryce. "And the TEMPUS Project is similar."

"TEMPUS?" Zac asked.

"The name we gave the project," Emilee said. "Temporal Energy Manipulation Portal Usage System."

"You lost me," Zac said.

"'Tempus' means 'time' in Latin. But for us, it's also an acronym."

"Then how does it work? I heard you say 'portal' or something. I didn't see any kind of a portal."

"It's not exactly what you think," his dad said. "It uses wormholes to travel from one place in time to another."

"Wormholes?" He raised his eyebrows. "You told me to keep an open mind, but you're not making it easy. You're talking about wormholes and portals… my science teacher said those are just theories."

Bryce slid the black, pen-like object on the table toward Zac, the same one he had found in the glass case embedded in the concrete wall. "Recognize this?"

Zac picked it up. It felt light in his hand, and the metal was cold. He studied the small strip where there had once been lights. It was dark.

"That's how we open one up," continued Bryce. "Using that. We call it a Wand. Wormhole Activation Network Device."

Emilee held out her hand to receive the Wand, and Zac passed it to her. "When you used it, you opened up a wormhole. It took you back in time somehow when you must have pressed this button on top."

She pressed the button. Nothing happened.

"See?" Zac said, looking at her. "You're still here; you didn't travel back in time."

"That's not how the Wand works," Bryce said. "It's kind of complicated, but the system has built-in checks and balances. It regulates travel by not allowing someone to just press it and open up a wormhole anywhere. To create a wormhole, you need a tremendous source of energy. Ours is in the room you saw last night."

A look of realization crossed Zac's face. "You mean the blue pentagon? I was standing on that when I pressed it."

"Exactly. So you activated it and leapt into the past," Bryce said. "I noticed the path behind the bookcase was open and checked the computer. I noticed a large energy spike, so I got worried. Either something had gone wrong, or someone had used the machine without being authorized to do so."

Zac nodded. "Okay, so if those Wand things let people jump around in time, aren't you worried that just anyone can break in and take one and use it?"

Dr. Ryger shook his head. "Even if someone were to find a Wand, it shouldn't work."

"Well, it did for me."

"But it *shouldn't* have," his dad continued. "As a safeguard, all of the Wands have sensors on the top that can only be activated by a unique user's fingerprint. That's why, when you press down, it makes it work. It also prevents people from using one if it's not theirs, like if someone from another time period somehow obtained it. It would be useless to them. But what baffles me is that the one you used wasn't registered to any user."

"What is it?"

"It's a prototype. Technically, it shouldn't work for anyone. It's not programmed to."

Bryce held up the Wand. "I agree. I've been trying to figure it out, and I've been analyzing it, but I have no idea why it worked for you, Zac." He shook his head. "There is no logical reason why this thing should be functioning for you. But it does. Maybe it's a malfunction or something. I need to figure it out."

Zac sat back in his chair, soaking it all in. Time travel. Was it truly possible?

"So that Wand took me back in time? To when?"

His dad sat forward. "I have a hypothesis," he said. "We usually program a place for the wormhole to open. But when you used it, we hadn't done so. I think that since you were somehow able to activate the device, it took you to the earliest date in your past."

"The day I was born," Zac said in realization.

"Yes," Dr. Ryger said. "Bryce was able to look at the program and discern where the wormhole opened up, and he followed you through it. That's why he was there." He looked at Bryce, thankfulness in his eyes. "I sent him to get you."

Zac slid the newspaper back toward himself. "So it really is me in this picture from the day I was born," he said, looking closely at it. "That's me in the past." He smiled in awe at the fact. "Wow. That's so cool."

The room was quiet. "Um, not necessarily," Emilee said. "We think it could actually be a big problem."

Zac looked puzzled. "What do you mean?"

"You might have changed things," she said.

EIGHT

"Changed things?" Zac said. "What do you mean? Everything's the same as far as I can tell."

Bryce shifted in his seat and scratched his forehead. "This is where things get a little tricky," he said. "You see, the few of us who have been in the program have been trained in how not to interfere with things. How to observe and gather data. We all know the rules."

"The rules?"

"The rules of time travel that we've established at TEMPUS," Bryce continued. "There are certain things you can and can't do."

"Like what?"

"Well, the biggest rule is that we can't interfere with the natural course of history. We have to let things happen the way they originally do... er... did."

Dr. Ryger spoke up. "The reason I built TEMPUS is to provide us with a way of observing the past, no matter how distant.

We can learn things that can affect our future for the better. But we can't go in and change the past."

"Why not?" Zac asked. "What's so bad about fixing things that went wrong in the past?"

Bryce leaned into the table. "Let's use a classic example. Killing Hitler." Zac nodded in understanding. "You know that Hitler killed millions of innocent people, how he invaded countries and caused untold death and destruction, right?"

"Right."

"So assume someone decides that they will build a time machine to go back and kill Hitler before he becomes powerful and can cause all that pain. Sounds good so far, right?" Zac nodded. "Okay, but here's the problem. Let's say the person who built the time machine succeeds. They go back and they kill Hitler. It's a perfect ending, right?"

"Yeah," Zac said. "All those people were saved."

"Wrong," Bryce said. "It can't possibly work. Because the *reason* the person built the time machine was *so that* he could go back and destroy Hitler. Now, with Hitler dead, his future self wouldn't have a reason to create a time machine. So his future self would never *build* that time machine, and he would never go back in time. It's called a paradox."

"You lost me," Zac said, shaking his head. Why wouldn't it be possible to just go erase someone from history? It sounded like it should work. "What about all those people that wouldn't have died?"

"Don't you see?" his dad said. "It can't happen."

"I don't get it," Zac said.

"Let me try explaining it a different way," Emilee said, taking a deep breath. "Okay, forget about the whole reason for building the machine and the paradox situation. Assume that one of us uses TEMPUS to go back and change things. Maybe it's major, maybe it's minor, but *something* has changed." She brushed a strand of black hair away from her eyes, but she continued looking down at the table while she talked, letting her hands do much of the talking for her. "If you change something, the effects could be small, but they could also be huge. Let's say you *do* go back in time and get rid of a dictator. You may have saved a lot of other lives and prevented something bad from happening, but in doing so, there were unintended consequences."

"Like what?" Zac asked.

"Like, maybe now, a new person rises up in the place of the dictator that was killed. And this person is *worse* than the one you got rid of. He causes far more suffering and death. Or he gives rise to other changes that affect a wider scope of people."

"So it's a no-win situation," Zac said.

"Possibly," Emilee continued. "We can't know for sure if we do change things, because changing one thing in the past can alter the course of our whole future."

"So wait," Zac interrupted. "You think I changed something by going back in time last night? But I didn't do anything."

"According to *you*, you didn't," Bryce said.

"I didn't," Zac said. "That picture proves it. My dad would have remembered it not being there beforehand if it wasn't."

His dad sighed. "Not necessarily." He put his head in his hands, trying to figure out how to best explain the situation. "There are two possibilities here, Zac. Either you're right, and that photo was *always* there all along, or it wasn't."

"Huh?"

"What I mean is, by going back in time, you might have now altered history and *this* is how it now happened," he said, tapping the picture. "We wouldn't remember if it was anything different, because now *this* is our history. This is what people remember."

Zac shook his head. "I don't see how my being in a picture changed anything."

"It's not the picture," Bryce said. "It's what you said or did. You went over to those cars to check on the people in them. Maybe that's how it always happened, and back on the day you were born, your future self was there. But it could also be that you did something that changed us here today."

"But I—"

"It could have been someone you talked to, something you said... anything, really," Bryce said. "But the point is there's no way for us to really know. It's all a theory. You dad calls it the Time Wound Theory."

"Time Wound? Like an injury?"

"Think of it like this," Emilee said. "When you get a cut, what happens?"

Zac paused. "I bleed," he said.

"Right. So the theory is that if we cause some sort of change in the past, the changes are like a cut. And the effects 'bleed' down throughout the course of history. By the time they reach us, it's like a scab has formed and it's a permanent part of our time as we know it."

Zac nodded. "I think I get it, sort of. So how can we know if I changed anything?"

"We can't," his dad said. "This is our history right now. Chances are you probably didn't change anything. Like you said, you didn't do much. But we're telling you this because if you're going to be a part of the project, you're going to have to understand the ramifications of time travel and causality."

"Wait," Zac said, sitting up, "part of the project? You mean I'll be working with you? With... what is it... TEMPUS?"

Dr. Ryger shifted uneasily. "We discussed it as a possibility this morning, if you should ever find out," he said. He picked up a pencil and began tapping it on the table. "For some unknown reason, that prototype Wand you found responded to you. And we don't know why." He stopped the tapping and looked around the room at Bryce and Emilee. "But we need to know why this happened, because if the technology isn't perfected, it could mean anyone can use it. And the results of a Wand getting into the wrong hands could be disastrous."

"So here's my idea," Bryce said. "We'll train you, and you can use this Wand until we're able to set you up with one of your own, one that is uniquely programmed to recognize you as the user."

"If this is some kind of joke—" Zac said, hesitating.

"No joke," Bryce said. "I'll take you and train you. I'll show you what TEMPUS is all about. And if you still want to, you can be a part of the group."

"The group? Who else is there besides you guys?"

Bryce stood up and pushed his chair in. "Let's go meet them," he said.

Bryce led Zac down the concrete corridor and toward the room with the blue pentagon. When they arrived, it was lit up this time, a brilliant white light illuminating everything.

"Welcome to TEMPUS," Bryce said. "Here is where we do our thing. Here is where the impossible happens." He smiled.

The air was filled with a loud humming noise, and the floor began to vibrate.

"Stay here," Bryce said, nodding toward the glass that surrounded the blue light. "Looks like he's coming back."

"Who?"

"Rock," Bryce said. "He went to collect some data for us. Watch this."

The light inside the glass cage flickered, and then bright flashes pulsated as loud popping noises filled the air. Zac's teeth tingled as if electrical impulses were emanating from the source. He pushed his fingers against his teeth.

"Got fillings?" Bryce said, straining to be loud enough to be heard over the whirr of the machine.

"Yeah," Zac said. "Is that normal?"

Bryce nodded. "It's just the resonant frequency. You get used to it. I don't even feel it anymore."

"What is it?" Zac asked. He was nearly yelling now, the machine was so loud.

Bryce pointed at the pentagon, where it looked like the form of a person was materializing. "There's a tremendous amount of energy coming into this room right now. That's why we're underground; this room is surrounded by concrete," he said. "What you're seeing is the wormhole opening back up, bringing Rock back."

The lights grew dim and stopped flickering. There was a pause as a sense of anticipation hung in the air. With a loud hiss, the glass door swung open, and Rock stepped out, careful to keep his balance.

"Man, I love that," Rock said, rubbing his face and smiling. "What a rush." He was tall and muscular, with dark skin. The muscles seemed to practically erupt from his arms and legs.

"Rock works with TEMPUS?" Zac asked. "But how——"

Rock stepped forward, extending his hand to shake Zac's. "How can a jock be working with a science team?" he said, finishing Zac's question. "You know, just 'cause I'm tough doesn't mean I can't think. I'm lucky enough to have brains *and* brawn." He smiled, and Zac realized that Rock wasn't offended at his question. Rock turned to Bryce. "So you guys decided to bring him in and tell him after all?" He walked over to a notebook that was in a plastic file holder on the wall and began writing in it furiously.

"Actually, he came to us," Bryce said. "We're going to train him."

Rock smiled. "Right on," he said. "I could use someone else to have my back out in the field." He handed the notebook to Bryce. "I got the intel we need. Call it in to the authorities. I think we can stop anything else from happening."

"Thanks," Bryce said. "Hey, do you mind showing Zac around while I go take care of this?"

"Sure," Rock said, "and do you want me to take him through the training scenario, too?" His face grew serious.

"No, I'll..." Bryce trailed off. "I'll do it tomorrow."

Rock shook his head in astonishment. "Okay. But you can't keep doing this to yourself. Are you ever gonna tell the Doc—"

"No," Bryce interrupted. "And neither are you. That's between us."

"Okay," Rock said. "Cause if the Doc knew, I don't think he'd be wanting you to do the training with Zac here."

"I'll be fine," Bryce said. "It's just an observation." He turned to leave and went up the ramp, Rock staring at him.

After he was gone, Zac asked, "What's the observation? Why don't you want Bryce to do it?"

Rock snapped back into the present. "Huh? Oh, the training. Yeah, I can't tell you anything about that. But a while ago, Bryce told me something about his past that he doesn't want me to tell anyone else. Not even your dad. And I'm not going to ruin his trust."

"I understand," Zac said.

"But you know, he might tell you if you ask right. He doesn't trust many people. He and I go way back."

Zac nodded. "Hey, I think I remember seeing you around at school a long time ago... You won a lot of medals in track and field. Roderick, was it?"

"Whoa," Rock said. "Nobody calls me Roderick but my mom. But yeah," he said. "Bryce told the Doc I was looking for a job, so your dad took a chance with me. I'm glad he did."

Zac paced around the room, looking at everything for the first time in the light. It seemed so different, yet still as mysterious as before.

"So where should I start?" Rock asked. "They tell me you already know about the wormhole manipulator here. How was your first time?"

Zac stared through the glass frame surrounding the platform. "Not too pleasant," he said.

"Did you puke?"

Zac looked up, embarrassed. "Yeah. Twice."

Rock laughed. "Everyone pukes the first time."

"What were you just doing, writing things down a few minutes ago?"

"That?" Rock said. "Oh, that's just part of what we do for the project. We observe and collect information. How much did your dad tell you?

"Nothing yet," Zac said. "They just got me really freaked out that I might have disrupted human history, that's all."

Rock waved it off. "It's fine. And besides, if you did, is anything here really bad or different?"

"No."

"Then it isn't worth worrying about, is it?" Rock walked down the other hallway, toward the computer Zac had seen the night before. "Want me to explain how it works?"

"Sure," Zac said. He surveyed the surroundings. He saw the small enclosure where he had found the Wand, but it was empty. "So how do you know where to go?"

"You mean where the wormhole opens up and spits us out?" he said. "That's kind of technical. Even I can't understand that.

Bryce and Emilee helped the Doc work on the program, so they understand it a bit better. Basically, it's sort of like GPS, but in time. The program can pinpoint some coordinates where it opens the hole up, but we can't be as exact as a building or anything, just a general area. So usually we set the coordinates for a field or something open. That way, you don't just suddenly appear in front of people, scaring them." He laughed. "Although one time, we messed up and I started out in the middle of a freeway. Almost got myself killed."

Zac thought for a moment, staring at the computer screen with all the bits of data he couldn't comprehend. "But there was no way for you to get killed, was there? I mean, you would've just been teleported or wormholed back, right?"

Rock's eyes got wide. "Man, I wish. No, you can die. Your physical body is there, in the past. You can get injured there just like anywhere else."

"So has anyone gotten killed yet?" Zac asked. "I mean, have you known anybody to go back and die while they were time-travelling?"

Rock fell silent. "Yeah, there was one. Never came back."

"But you have a time portal," Zac said. "Why not travel to right when the person left and tell them not to go?"

Rock shook his head. "It's all complicated. They programmed the computer to have all of these specifications and rules and junk, all to try and eliminate possible paradoxes. So for example, when I open a wormhole and go back to the past, if something bad happens, I can't just return to the time before I leave and tell myself not to go. The machine won't allow it."

"How does it prevent you?"

"It has parameters built in that only let you return here about five minutes after you left. So that way, no matter what, we avoid messing things up. It's like a 'buffer zone' of sorts."

"That's weird."

"Tell me about it," Rock said, getting up and walking back into the main room. "I could be gone for an entire day and when I get back here to our time, only about five minutes will have passed. It really messes with your body's clock. That's why you're gonna need *this*," he said, holding up a syringe.

"What's that?" Zac asked.

"Just a little something the Doc had developed by a friend of his. Uses nanotechnology to regulate things in your body." He jabbed the needle into Zac's left arm, right below his shoulder.

"Ow!" Zac said.

"Sorry, man," Rock said. "But this should make things better all around. Now when you travel, your body will adapt better. Trust me. No more puking." He pulled the needle out. "Probably."

Zac rubbed his shoulder. It tingled, and it felt as if something were spreading up his arm, cold and icy.

"That feeling will go away soon," Rock said. "Some people feel like they're getting a sudden fever, like Emilee did. Some people feel like there's ice creeping up their veins."

Zac walked over to where Rock had written in the notebook. "You said that you were collecting data or observing something. What's that all about?"

"Oh, that," Rock said. "Did your dad tell you how we don't use TEMPUS to mess with the past?"

"Yeah," Zac said, leaning against the concrete wall. He scratched his head. The icy feeling in his arm was subsiding now. "He said you just observe the past, get a better picture of history or something like that."

"Right," Rock said. "When the Doc told me we couldn't change the past, I figured there's no point in having time travel. But here's the cool thing: we can observe the past to affect the present *and* future."

"How?" Zac said. He paced the room, walking around the wormhole platform now, watching the swirling liquid underneath the glass floor. "If you can't change anything, that doesn't make any sense."

"No, it totally does if you think about it. Okay, I just got back from my mission, right?"

"Yeah. What does that have to do with anything?"

"There was an armored car robbery yesterday. The two guys driving the armored car were shot at point-blank range. Had bullet-proof vests and everything, but the criminals had better weapons. Dangerous ones."

"So you time-travelled to stop them from getting killed?"

"No. Remember, you can't change things. It might mess up things today. But I was able to go back and witness the getaway, get descriptions of the criminals, memorize their license plate and vehicle description, and get other data on them. And right now," he pointed up toward the ceiling, "Bryce is on the phone with the authorities giving them the information. Soon, you'll probably see it on the news that they'll get the guys who held up the car."

A slight smile crossed Zac's face. "So now, those guys can't hold up any more armored vehicles."

"Right. They won't be able to hurt anyone else. And the police can find out where those weapons came from, too."

If this were true, then it was perfect. Zac could finally find a way to do what he dreamed. Ever since he could remember, he wanted to be a police officer or in law enforcement somehow. But it always made him a bit apprehensive when he considered it. He hated confrontation. He wasn't tough or strong like Rock.

Yet deep down, he felt like it was what he was meant to do. Maybe it had something to do with how his mom was killed. He never really knew. But if he could help people with TEMPUS, maybe he would be doing something worthwhile with his life.

They were interrupted by the sound of footsteps running down the concrete pathway. Emilee entered the room. "The authorities found them," she said.

"Already?" Rock asked.

"Yeah," she said, walking over to him. He gave her a quick kiss on the cheek. "Your description led them right to their doorstep. Great work. Let's go out and celebrate." She looked over and saw Zac. "You wanna come too?"

"No, that's okay," he said. "I don't do so well in crowds."

Rock didn't buy his excuse. "Oh, come on, man. We're going to be working together now; let's go get something to eat. Get to know each other."

"Seriously," Zac said. "I appreciate it, but maybe another time."

"Okay," Rock said. "Suit yourself." They began walking back to the main level of the office. "It's probably best anyway. If you're going to be doing the training exercise tomorrow, I'd go home and get some rest. You're going to need it."

Emilee had a stunned look on her face. "Dr. Ryger's going to make him do the training observation?" She looked at Zac with concern in her eyes. "But he's already experienced a time leap. Shouldn't that be enough?"

"Guess not. The Doc wants everyone to go through the same training. Even his own son."

"You're not going to take him, are you?" she asked.

"No. Bryce said he will."

"Good," Emilee said. "I don't know how Bryce is able to do this so many times, but I remember what happened to you after the first time you went. It changed you."

"I think that's the point," Rock said. He patted Zac on the shoulder, the same one he injected the needle into, and Zac winced. "Good luck tomorrow, man. Let me know how it goes."

NINE

Zac sat in front of the television, eating some popcorn and putting his feet up on the coffee table, something his dad always hated. *Back to the Future* was on, the scene where Marty McFly meets his dad as a teenager in the 1955 diner. He laughed to himself. Tomorrow, he would be travelling to someplace in the past himself, only he'd be using some glowing platform and a handheld device instead of a DeLorean.

The DeLorean would be cooler, he thought. Who wouldn't want to drive a car where the doors opened by spreading up like an eagle's wings?

His dad walked in the room, and Zac quickly took his feet off the coffee table. "You know, I always loved this movie," he said.

"Imagine that," Zac said, tossing another handful of popcorn into his mouth. "I bet you love how Rock calls you 'Doc,' too."

"Actually," his dad said, smiling, "I kind of do. Makes me feel like Doc Brown in the movie. Only I think I have better hair."

57

Zac laughed and offered his dad some popcorn. They never really sat down like this anymore. Zac could tell something was bothering him.

"You know, Zac, I never meant to lie to you about anything."

"Then why did you?" Zac asked. "I wish you and Bryce just told me the truth the other night."

Dr. Ryger looked down at the carpet. "You weren't supposed to hear what we talked about," he said. "But for what it's worth, I'm sorry. I don't want my own son thinking I don't care about him. That's why this is so hard for me."

"What is?"

"Letting you join the program. Zac, I don't feel comfortable with you doing this."

Zac sat up and set the bowl of popcorn aside. "What do you mean? You're just going to tell me I can't go now?"

"No," his dad said, "not at all. But I'm hesitant." He breathed deep and looked at Zac. "Son, time travel isn't a game or a playground."

"I know," Zac said, irritation in his voice. "I'm not stupid." He rolled his eyes.

"I never said you were. What I mean is..." He paused to gather his thoughts. "What I mean is that time travel is dangerous. You can die if you don't know what you're doing. It's like going into a foreign land. If you're not ready—"

"I understand," Zac said. "Rock told me about it. I'll be careful."

"Rock told you? What did he say?"

Zac shrugged. "Nothing. He just said that someone has already died doing this."

His dad nodded. "And I've never forgiven myself. It was the last time I went back in time myself. I wish I could fix things, but I was careless."

"What happened?" Zac asked, reaching down for the television remote. He muted the TV.

"It doesn't matter right now," Dr. Ryger said. "I think he's forgiven me. Luckily, Rock's a nice kid. He knew that he and his brother were taking a big risk by volunteering for the program."

"His brother? But he didn't say anything about that."

Dr. Ryger smiled. "He probably wouldn't. He's got a pure heart. I'm sure he didn't say anything because he doesn't want you to have a tainted image of me. But I was at fault. We were observing an event, and I wanted to get closer to what was happening. Rock's brother got killed while using TEMPUS." He stared off into space, thinking.

"So you've used it, too?"

"Only a couple of times," Dr. Ryger replied. "Because of the tremendous amount of energy used when a person travels through the wormhole, it can wreak havoc on the traveler's body. That's why I've enlisted younger people in the program. Their body can handle it better."

A long silence hung in the air. Zac was at a loss of what to say about Rock's brother.

"I guess I just don't want to see the same thing happen to you," he said. "I couldn't bear to lose you too. You're all I've got left."

Zac stared at the television screen, avoiding eye contact with his dad. He knew what his dad was referring to, and he didn't want to think about it and start tearing up.

"I know what you're thinking, Zac," he said. "I think I know why you want to do this, deep down." Zac looked up and met his gaze. "And you can't do it. It won't work. You can't save her and bring her back."

Zac looked away. He was careful not to say anything or even hint at it. He didn't want to get his hopes up, but deep down he wondered if maybe, just maybe, if he could learn to use the technology well enough, he could change things.

"Why not?" Zac asked, his voice cracking with sadness.

"It doesn't work that way," his dad said. "It's against the rules. You can't change things. We talked about this."

"But who made the rules?" Zac said. "You? If it's your time machine or whatever, then why can't you do what you want with it?"

"Son, I told you," he said, speaking quietly to counter Zac's rising tension, "there are natural laws that govern time. I know it's not easy to accept. I had trouble accepting it. But we can't bring your mom back."

Zac turned to look at him, his eyes now red with tears. "Did you ever try?"

Dr. Ryger was silent. After a moment, he spoke. "No," he said.

"Then how do you know it's not possible?"

"I just know."

"Bull." Zac shook his head. His dad didn't try because he was afraid. But Zac wasn't. If he could, he'd go back in time and confront the killer, stopping him. All he needed to do was find out where and when it took place. His dad never talked about it and refused to put the death date on the gravestone. "Did Mom know about your secret project? Or did you lie to her, too?"

"I worked on TEMPUS *after* she died," his dad said. "And don't think for a minute that I don't want her back. I miss her every day I wake up. I miss coming home to see her, and I miss telling her about my day. But things have changed; we have to accept what's happened in the past." He sighed. "Some things are just meant to be."

Anger rose inside Zac. "How can you just say that? 'Some things are just meant to be'? So you're saying that Mom is just *meant* to be dead?"

"Maybe. I don't know."

Zac got up off the couch and stood. "I refuse to believe that. And you know what? If I can find a way to go back and save her, I'll do it. And nothing, not even you, can stop me."

Dr. Ryger sighed. "Okay, Zac. But I'm telling you, you can't change the past. It's already happened and done."

"We'll see about that," Zac said. He went to his room and slammed the door. Meant to be dead. How stupid was that? He turned off the light and threw himself on the bed. All he had to do was find out what date his mom died, and he could fix everything. He just had to think.

He was too young to remember it all. All he could recall was a man in the crowd coming up to him and grabbing him, and then there was a struggle and yelling, and the next thing he knew, his mom was dead. The man who killed her had to have gotten away.

When he had his chance, Zac would make sure that if he couldn't save his mom, he could at least bring the killer to justice.

The next day, Zac and Bryce stood inside the underground room, facing the crystal-clear glass door.

"You think you're ready?" Bryce asked.

Zac shook his head. "No," he said. "But I guess I'm as ready as I'll ever be. Do we go now?" He took a step toward the platform.

"Wait a minute," he said. "We need someone to run the program, to set the coordinates." He looked down the hallway and called out to someone. "Chen!"

A guy with black, buzzed hair came down the hallway. He had on a red college t-shirt and blue jeans that were faded and torn.

He looked slightly older than Bryce and Rock, probably in graduate school.

"Yeah?" he said, but stopped when he saw Zac. "Oh, hey. Nice to meet you. Sorry I wasn't here yesterday. I had class."

"Nice to meet you, too," Zac said. "Are Emilee and Rock here?"

"Not this early," Chen said. "Usually they come in later. I'm always up early because I have a class at seven. Might as well get an early start. I was just working on the system."

"We need you to set the parameters for the training leap."

Chen's face grew serious. "Oh," he said. "Dr. Ryger's still making him do it?"

"Apparently," Bryce said.

"You guys are making me nervous," Zac said. "What's the big deal about where we're going?"

"Um, it's not so much the *where* as the *when*," Chen said. "But I'm sure Bryce can explain it to you when you're there. I'll set it up so you have some time to talk for a little while."

"Not too long," Bryce said. "And you're going to have to put us in the middle of the city, but just try to make it in an open place."

"Will do," Chen said, offering a thumbs-up. "Let me go back to the computer and get it ready. Just give me two minutes, and you can do your thing."

"Thanks," Bryce said, and they watched him walk down the hall. He turned to Zac. "Okay, before we do this, I have to reiterate the rules with you."

"I already know," Zac said, "we can't change anything, right?"

"True," Bryce said, standing back as the glass door gently swung open with a hissing sound. The blue pentagon grew brighter and started to hum. "Whenever possible, you never go alone. That's why I'm going with you now."

"Is my dad going to be here?" Zac said.

"Not today," Bryce said. "He pretty much runs things upstairs. We'll be fine. And here's the most important thing: if you ever are in a place in your own past where you might see yourself, you *must* avoid your past self at all costs. That way, you can't give yourself any information or warnings or anything. It could cause a wound in time, but we wouldn't know it."

"Got it," Zac said, taking a deep breath. Bryce swept his arm and motioned for Zac to walk onto the platform. He was really going to do this; he was going to travel through time. His heart pounded in excitement. He couldn't wait to get there and look around, see the sights and find out what was so mysterious about this training exercise. It was probably just some joke to scare him. His dad probably put them up to it to discourage him from going.

He smiled, stepped on, and Bryce followed. The door closed behind them.

"Here's the Wand," Bryce said, handing it to him. He pulled out his own Wand, identical to the one Zac held. Bryce pointed to the row of lights on the side. "These lights here tell you if it's working. They're on a sort of timer. The power in them can't last forever, so make sure the lights don't go out."

The look on Zac's face grew serious. "What happens if the lights go out?"

Bryce stared straight ahead. "Just don't let them. And don't lose your Wand. No one else should be able to use it, but we don't know for sure, since the one you have let *you* activate it somehow."

"Got it," Zac said, squaring his shoulders. "How do we get back?"

Bryce pointed to the top where he was placing his thumb. "Same way we leave. Pressing it opens the wormhole and allows us to travel through. Pressing it again re-opens the wormhole and brings us back to the origin. Right here."

"Okay," Zac said, full of excitement. "Just tell me when."

"In a minute. One thing: don't press it to return back here until I tell you to. Ready?"

"Ready!" The machine hummed.

Bryce closed his eyes. "Go!"

Simultaneously, Zac and Bryce pressed down on their devices. Zac felt the floor vibrate under him, and his whole body seemed to feel as if waves were pulsating against him. A deafening sound filled his ears, and everything blurred.

As quickly as it had started, it was over. Zac didn't feel the effects as badly as he had the last time. He stumbled a bit, and was quickly pushed by a passerby on the sidewalk.

All around him was a sea of people, moving down the sidewalk like mice through a maze. Zac looked to his left and saw Bryce standing against a building.

"We're here," Bryce said.

TEN

Zac made his way over to Bryce. "So where are we?" he asked. "This isn't our city, is it?"

"I can't tell you that yet," he said. "But I can tell you that we can travel to different locations in time, too. It's part of the training exercise. I'll tell you what, let's go get something to drink and have a seat for a while. I could use a rest."

They walked down the sidewalk as cabs screamed by, picking up and dropping off their fares. Massive skyscrapers stretched into the sky, surrounding them on all sides. The morning sun reflected off of their surfaces, and Zac had to get his bearings after looking up at them for so long. He wasn't used to seeing so many gigantic buildings.

"Wow," he said. "This is so much different than back home."

They came to a sidewalk café and sat down on the metal chairs.

"So you've done this before?" Zac asked.

"Yeah," Bryce answered. "A couple of times."

Zac was still reeling from the idea that he was somewhere in the past. He didn't know when, but he was sure it wasn't a dream.

"I'm still just in total shock," Zac said. "Don't you get excited every time you do this?"

"Usually," Bryce said. He was quieter than normal. Zac decided to tone down his enthusiasm.

"Do you know how this all actually works?" Zac asked. "The science behind it? I'd ask my dad, but I think he would get too technical."

Bryce nodded. "A little," he said. "I mean, I can't explain it as well as a physicist like your dad can. But basically, the Wand you have has the ability to use the energy on the platform to transport you through the wormhole. It sort of charges the atoms in your body, giving them the power to travel that huge distance. That's why you feel those vibrations. There's so much energy passing through your body, it's like you're being electrocuted."

Zac thought back to his initial experience and how painful it was. Whatever Rock injected him with must have helped. "But how is this possible? How can it actually *work*?"

Bryce thought for a moment. "The best explanation I can think of is to think of it in terms of dimensions. *Time* is the fourth dimension. If you'd told people more than a century ago that we would be able to travel vertically from the earth, into the sky and space with airplanes and space shuttles, they wouldn't have believed you. But science advanced to the point where travel in the third dimension was possible."

"And so now we can travel in the fourth dimension?" Zac asked.

"In short, yes. We use the Wand to activate the wormhole, and that's the gist of it."

66

"But how can a wormhole do that? Does one just suddenly appear?"

Bryce shook his head. "It's not like that," he said. It's more of a *bending* of space and time. Here— I have an idea." He picked up a straw off the sidewalk. "Okay, look at this little ant that has found his way up the table. Let's pretend this little guy is you."

"I'd rather be a spider."

Bryce smiled and grabbed a napkin from a nearby table that was abandoned. "This napkin has a line printed on it. That line represents the flow of time." He traced his finger on it. The ant was starting to crawl across the napkin, and was moving around the line. "This line, like time, has a starting point and an ending point. Right now, where that ant is standing is his 'present.' Like us, he just goes along that timeline, from start to finish."

"Okay," Zac said. "I get that time is a line, but what about the wormhole? How does that work?"

Bryce held up the straw. "Here's the wormhole. When we use it, it takes us from our present..." He placed it on the napkin where the ant was, and the ant crawled inside it. He bent the straw so that it went up in an arc over the line to a different point earlier on it. "It takes us from our present to the past, somewhere else on the time line, like this." The ant crawled out, ending up at a different place on the line. "It's the same thing for us. And we can just use the wormhole to get back to our start."

Zac nodded in understanding, and the ant crawled away.

"Let me ask you something," Zac said. "When I saw my dad in the past, I talked to him, and I didn't change anything. So what's the big deal?"

"What did you talk about?"

"It was weird, really," Zac continued. "I got to see myself as a baby. My dad told me what he was naming me... well, the baby-me. Isaac, my full name."

"Isaac?"

"Yeah," Zac said, watching people pass by. A man hailed a cab and jumped in. "He told me long ago that he named me after Isaac Asimov because he loved the science fiction Asimov wrote."

"That's cool. I was named after a guy in a donut shop."

"Seriously?" Zac smiled.

"Yep," Bryce said. "My mom got pregnant pretty young. I never met my dad. He was a deadbeat, I guess. But anyway, one day she walked into a donut shop and the guy who worked there was just really nice to her and talked to her. She ended up going there every morning, and she said they'd talk about life. It was like they were best friends."

"Was she in love with him?"

Bryce shook his head. "No, no, it wasn't anything like that. It definitely wasn't a romantic love. The way she talked about him, it was like he was the kindest person in the world to her. She used to say that he made her feel so worthwhile that she knew he was sent from God to give her hope that everything was going to be okay with her new baby. He encouraged her." He smiled. "And so she named me after him as a way to say thanks."

It was interesting, Zac thought. One person made such a huge difference in another life that it carried down through time. Like the Time Wound theory, but the opposite. Good can bleed through, too. So why couldn't he go back and save his own mom? Wouldn't good come from that?

"My mom never got to tell him what she named me," Bryce said. "She got a new job and moved right around the time she gave birth to me. Even before she died, she still talked about him."

Zac was still fixated on his own mom. "So do you think it's possible to change things?"

Bryce shook his head. "No. I mean, there are two lines of thought on this. One is what your dad already explained, that it creates a wound in time that scabs over into something new and different."

"What's the other theory?"

"It would be the idea that, for example, the picture of you in that newspaper was always like that. You were there all along; you just lived through it right now, but the *future* you always did that. There was a funny sketch on television once," he said, starting to laugh. "It had Abraham Lincoln build a time machine, and he saw how John Wilkes Booth kills him at Ford's Theater. So Lincoln uses his time machine to go back to when Booth was a kid, and he tries to kill him.

"He fails, but he keeps going back to kill Booth at different stages in his life. Finally, Booth is an adult and says that he's had it with this man who has been trying to kill him all his life, and he realizes it's been Lincoln, the president, who has been terrorizing him all along. So he kills Lincoln to protect his own life."

Zac laughed. "So by trying to prevent his own death, he *made* John Wilkes Booth want to kill him." It was funny to think about. "So what do you think?"

"Me?" Bryce said. "I don't know, but I just think we should follow the rules and not mess with time. We can't all change the things we don't like. But I'd say if anyone had a reason to change their past, it would be Emilee."

"Emilee? Why?"

Bryce grew quiet. "It's not for me to say. Let's just say she's had it rougher than most. It's understandable why she gravitates to a strong guy like Rock, though."

There was a loud, low whining sound in the air. A large shadow passed over them, and Zac looked up to see an airplane flying lower than he'd ever seen before.

"Here we go," he heard Bryce whisper, remaining motionless.

Zac's eyes followed the plane as it descended lower, and that was when he noticed it heading toward a tall building.

"Bryce!" he yelled. "That's the World Trade Center! That plane's going to—"

There was a loud explosion that echoed through the air, the sound waves reverberating through the buildings on the streets. Panic ensued as people screamed, watching the plume of smoke and flames lick the side of the building, radiating in a cloud that expanded outward.

Bryce refused to look up.

"We have to get out of here!" Zac yelled. "No, wait! The second plane! We still have time to tell someone about the second one! We need to find a phone. Or something! We can—"

"No!" Bryce said firmly. "We can't do anything. It's already done."

"Don't you get it?" Zac said, running into the street. Smoke was rising from the tower, and people everywhere were straining to see what had happened. Zac wanted to yell that there was a second one on its way, but he was shocked that Bryce just sat there.

There were still people in those towers. People who were dying of smoke inhalation and who were burning in the intense heat. And soon, another plane was going to hit the second tower, and they would both collapse into a pile of rubble unlike anything the world had seen.

The second tower. If Zac could get the message to them, they could get more people out this time. This time, less people would die. All he had to do was tell someone. But how?

He turned to Bryce. "Aren't you going to do something?" he asked. "You know how this ends up. We can save lives!" He moved in closer to Bryce, who told him to sit down. Zac refused.

Smoke filled the sky now, and Zac was horror-stricken. He remembered all of those phone calls he had heard in school. The ones his teacher played that were from answering machines of families who had lost loved ones in the towers.

The messages saying "goodbye" and "tell the kids I love them" and "I won't make it home." Zac stood, watching down the street with his hands on his head. He felt helpless, like he was one of the people he saw in all of the photos who stood and stared.

The entire time, Bryce sat, not even bothering to look in the direction of the turmoil. It was like he was numb to it all. Uncaring. Unsympathetic.

Zac stood, eyes transfixed on the tower as if seeing it for the first time in his life. He was far enough away that he was safe, but not so far removed that his mind didn't recall the videos he had seen of people who leapt to their deaths. Facing the choice of dying from what must have been unbearable heat and flames or by having their body crash into the pavement. He remembered the jumpers, images flowing into his mind.

He stood for what seemed like an eternity, helpless. Time seemed to slow down, though only about fifteen minutes had passed. And that was when the second plane hit.

The side of the tower erupted into a ball of flame and fury as he stood, horrified. It was instant death for those people. He thought of the children who were on board those planes, what must have been going through their minds moments before the plane hit, clinging to their parents in their last seconds on earth.

Bryce sat like a statue, his head propped up and resting on his hand. Zac stormed over and tried shaking him from his reverie.

"Dammit! We have to *do something!*" he screamed, getting in Bryce's face.

Bryce pulled him down into his chair. "*We can't!*" he said. "You don't get it, do you? Why do you think *this* is the training mission?"

Zac was breathing heavily now, still unable to calm himself down.

"Your dad wants us all to see that we can't change things. Don't you think I would if I could?"

"But you just sat here while it all happened," Zac said. "It's like you don't even care!"

"Don't tell me what I care about!" Bryce yelled. Zac was taken aback by the look of anger in his eyes, a fire he had never seen before. "I've seen this scene play out more than any other person in the program. Once is bad enough. Seeing it again and again has made nightmares seem like a cake walk."

Zac sat in silence. It had to be awful to see this again and again, knowing you were powerless to help. No wonder Bryce didn't even bother to look. He'd seen it before. Once was enough, seeing videos of it. But to see it again and again... in *real life*...

"Sorry," Zac said, calming down. "I didn't realize."

"It's fine," Bryce said. "It's almost time to leave anyway. We don't want to watch any more of this than we have to."

"So why doesn't anyone try to go back and alert the authorities about this?" Zac asked, treading lightly.

Bryce finally turned to Zac. "We can't break the rules. We can't change anything."

"But what can possibly be so bad about trying to stop this? What could possibly go wrong if we intervene?"

"We don't know," Bryce said. "Causality is a tricky thing, and since we don't know, we don't act." His calm demeanor was completely the opposite of the chaos in the streets.

People were screaming, crying. Zac heard someone yell. "Oh, God! They're jumping! Those people are jumping!" He closed his eyes and tried to hold his emotions in check.

"I want to go back," Zac said. "I want to return to the present."

"Soon," Bryce said. "But do you see why we're here? There is always something we want to change. Everyone has something, even I do. But we can't change every bad thing. It's impossible."

"But this is so big," Zac said, eyes full of tears. He tried to block out the sounds surrounding him.

"Yes, but it's filled with so many variables that we don't know what would happen if all those people survived."

"Those are *people*, not variables!"

"I know," Bryce said. "I agree. But there will come a point where every single one of us will want to use this ability of time travel to correct something. To stop something bad from happening. But we can't." He sighed. "We have to resist that temptation when it comes to us."

He held out his Wand. "But I agree with you. It's time to go. Ready?"

"Never more ready," Zac said, holding out the device and grasping it firmly in his fist like Bryce had shown him.

He placed his thumb on the top of the device and pushed down. As the world around him faded, he could hear the sirens and the screams of people.

ELEVEN

The world swirled back into focus. Zac could feel the platform below his feet, and the sensation of dizziness came and went much quicker than it had last time. He took a deep breath, steadied himself, and then opened his eyes.

Outside the wormhole chamber, the members of the TEMPUS Project waited. Emilee stood close to Rock's side, her hand touching his right arm. Chen stood off to the side, ear buds in his ears. Zac could see his dad coming down the concrete ramp, a concerned look on his face.

The chamber door opened, and everyone seemed to be waiting in expectation for Zac to say something. He stepped forward and handed his Wand to Bryce, who took it and put it in a case mounted to the wall. Each Wand belonged to a different user, and the spaces were labeled below them. Since they were all identical, it would be easy to grab the wrong one.

Bryce locked the case and handed the keys over to Dr. Ryger.

"How'd it go?" Rock asked.

"Same as always," Bryce said. "Same reaction, same questions everyone else had."

Dr. Ryger approached Zac and put a comforting hand on his shoulder. "You doing okay?" His eyes held a genuine look of concern.

Zac hesitated a moment, then recoiled. "How can you just let people watch that?" he asked. "You just throw me into a helpless situation like that? What's the point?"

"The point," his dad said, "is that we can't change things for reasons we won't always know or understand."

"Why not?" Zac asked with anger. "Why can't we change the fact that those buildings fell? Why can't we stop those people from jumping to their deaths?"

"He's right, man," Rock said. "I mean, I hated watching it, too. I wish I could still go back and do something. But listen to what your dad has to say."

"*This* ought to be good," Zac mumbled.

Dr. Ryger sat down on a nearby chair. "Zac, you time-traveled. Those people were already dead before you went there. Think of it this way. Yes, that day was tragic. Horrible. Devastating. But consider this." He paused, taking a breath. It was like he was preparing a monologue he had used several times before. "Because of those attacks, airport security and, well, security everywhere was heightened. More protocols were established, and government agencies began to collaborate for the first time to combine their intelligence information. With that, they caught a lot of other terrorists and prevented some other big attacks." Zac tried to interrupt, but he held up a finger. "Now, think about it: if we stopped those attacks, it would be good because all of those people would be alive. But then what?"

"What do you mean?" Zac asked. "Then they'd be alive, I guess."

"Here's what I mean," Dr. Ryger said. He shifted in his chair. "We don't really *know* what would be next. We *think* things would be fine. But maybe, because security was never heightened as a result of the attacks, something far worse got through. A terrorist cell got ahold of a dirty bomb, or a biological or chemical weapon. They unleash it on a city and it spreads, killing hundreds of thousands of people or more."

"That's just a giant 'what if?' that can never be proven or disproven."

"True," his dad replied. "But the point is we don't know what effect our changes would have. They could be better, or they could be worse. We just need to accept the fact that some things are meant to be."

Zac shook his head and looked around the room. Chen was awkwardly shuffling his feet. Clearly, he'd been fed this line too. Emilee wasn't making eye contact with anyone. If what Bryce said was right, her bitterness was probably growing each time his dad said some things were "meant to be" a certain way.

He still couldn't accept it. Maybe on a grand scale, saving three thousand lives would have too many repercussions. But one life? One small change? Doubtful.

Bryce came forward. "You know, Zac, I felt the same way before. But at TEMPUS, we *can* actually stop bad things from happening, and there are no repercussions. We observe, we report, and we prevent worse things from happening." He put a hand on Zac's shoulder. "We could use your help. I know you're the kind of guy who wants to do what is right; I've seen it in you. And while we might not be able to use time travel for the reasons we'd really like to, we can do a lot of good with the way we *do* use it."

"What do you say, Zac?" Emilee said. "Can you really go back to normal life after this?"

Zac was silent, letting the thoughts swirl through his head. So much was at stake. On the one hand, it would let him help people. In a sense, he would be participating in a form of law enforcement, a new form. But on the other hand, he'd have to observe a lot of tragedies. Tragedies he would want to prevent but wasn't allowed to interfere with. Could he do it?

"I'm not sure," Zac said. He tossed the idea back and forth in his head. The image of his mom dying flashed through his mind. What if this technology had been around back when his mom was killed? What if the killer had already committed another crime beforehand? A group like TEMPUS could have gotten information and had the killer arrested before he had a chance to shoot her. That would have definitely changed things for Zac. Could he do the same for others?

Dr. Ryger stood and started up the hallway toward the main office. "Well, you have a chance to think about it and let us know," he said.

"No," Zac said. His dad turned. "I don't need to think about it. I'll do it. I'm in."

Everyone around him smiled.

"Awesome," said Chen. "It'll be great to have someone else on the team."

Rock shook Zac's hand hard. He clasped the other arm around Zac, pulling him in and giving him a bear hug. "You made the right choice," he said. "I don't regret joining for a second."

Emilee stood off to the side, but she gave Zac a quick glance and half a smile. She was more distant than the others, but Zac didn't want to press her.

"So what's next?" Zac said.

"The next thing," Bryce said, "is for you to go home and get some rest. Tomorrow after school, you can come here and we can see if there's something you can do."

Zac found it difficult to sleep. His mind was filled with recurring images of the planes slamming into the buildings, the glass and flames radiating from the impact. The fact that he did nothing to stop it haunted him.

Yet he knew that was the purpose of the time leap. He was supposed to feel helpless. He was supposed to witness something so big he had no choice but to let it happen, to let its effects bleed through time and take shape. This way, when he was faced with smaller things he'd want to change, he would remember that it was impossible. It was against the rules of time travel.

He laughed to himself. A week ago, would he have foreseen himself lying in bed, pondering the rules of traveling through the space-time continuum?

His cell phone vibrated on the nightstand next to him. He read the caller ID and answered. "Hey, Bryce," he said. "What's up?"

"I was just calling to check in on you," Bryce said. "I remember having trouble sleeping after the first time, too. Let me guess: you can't sleep, either."

"Not at all," Zac said. He sat up and reached over, turning on the lamp next to his bed. "I just keep feeling... I don't know how to describe it."

"Guilty?" Bryce said.

"Yeah. I think that's exactly it."

"I know how you feel. But I think that's the other point of seeing what you saw."

"How?" Zac asked.

"Well," Bryce continued, "I think that now, because you feel so guilty and helpless, you'll have a desire to do what's right. You know you can't use the technology to affect the past."

"But I can use it to affect the future," Zac finished. It made sense. It did make him want to help others. "I just wish there was a way to do both."

He heard Bryce sigh. "You and me both, man. I think all of us have something we'd love to change."

Zac began to think of Emilee, her serious demeanor and her often forlorn gaze. Something had stolen her smile from her; she rarely seemed happy. Bryce said that if anyone had a reason to fix something, it would be her. But what could be worse than seeing a parent get killed?

"Can I ask you something?" Zac said.

"Shoot."

"Earlier today, you said something about Emilee. Something about her having a difficult life."

"Yeah," Bryce said, exhaling slowly. "You could say that."

Zac paused, unsure if he should press on. But he had to know. "What happened?" He knew this was probably something he shouldn't be asking, but what if he accidentally said something to her that would trigger bad memories? He didn't want any awkwardness between them.

"You knew she grew up in foster care, right?" Bryce asked.

"No."

"Yeah. To make a long story short, her stepfather was abusive. Physically, verbally, emotionally... it was horrible. He would lock her in a closet for an entire day while he was at work. More than once, he made her sleep outside in the snow with just a thin blanket. And there's a lot more I don't even want to go into."

Zac couldn't believe it. "How do you know this?"

"She told me," he said. "She and I dated for a while, back when the project first started. But things fell apart." He paused. "You need to promise me you won't say anything to her about this. But I think you should know, since you might be in the field with her tomorrow."

"Tomorrow?"

"Yeah. She's going to be with you on any observations you need to do. Just remember to listen to her. She knows what she's doing."

"Okay," Zac said, looking forward to spending some time with her. He wondered if she was just really good friends with Rock, or if there was something more there. Maybe she'd open up a bit with him.

"Good luck tomorrow," Bryce said. "And remember, as helpless as you might feel, you're still making a change. It just might not be the change you *want* to make."

After school, Zac stepped into the office building where TEMPUS was housed and nodded to the security guard. He walked down the hallway and saw Emilee sitting at the desk, waiting.

"Hey," he said, smiling. She looked down at the computer screen, her eyes not leaving the monitor.

"How was your day?" she asked.

"Fine. Nothing major," Zac said, shrugging. "So, what's on the agenda?" he asked. Despite the fact that an observation would mean something bad had happened, Zac secretly wanted to go on one.

"Only one thing," she said, staring at the monitor. "A little girl was kidnapped about three hours ago. We just found out."

"Is that a short enough time that we can go back and stop it from happening?" Zac asked. What kind of side-effects would that possibly have? A happy family?

"No," she replied. "We still can't interfere. But this is going to be critical to get the information as soon as we can. In cases like these, the first few hours are the most important." She turned the monitor off and pushed in her chair, walking toward the bookcase. She tugged it slightly and it rolled back, revealing the dark hallway that descended below. She continued down toward the base of operations. Zac followed.

"So tell me what to do," he said. He could feel the adrenaline surging through his body, his heart beating in anticipation. He felt like a secret spy on a mission, just like in the movies. Only this was real. He had to succeed. A kid's life depended on it.

"When we get down there, empty your pockets," she said. "We try not to take anything with us except the clothes we're wearing. That way, we can't accidentally leave anything behind." She came to the bottom of the incline and entered the room with the platform. It was faintly lit. She walked over to the case on the wall that housed the Wands and unlocked the case, hanging the keys on a nearby hook, and took two of them out. "Here's yours," she said, handing him the one he had used twice before. "Your dad's still engineering an official one that's designed to use your fingerprint. We don't want to use this one any more than we have to."

Zac weighed the Wand in his hand turned toward the platform, the place where a wormhole would soon open and pull him hours into the past. It was amazing, he thought, how from that one location he could go ten minutes or ten thousand years back in time. He walked toward the glass enclosure.

"Chen!" Emilee yelled. "Get it ready for us."

A voice from down the hallway echoed in compliance.

"Does he ever go, too?"

81

"All the time," Emilee said. "But we need someone to stay back in case there are complications."

"Complications?" Zac asked.

"Don't worry about it."

Zac watched her as she readied herself, standing outside the platform. She was so tense, so driven. He was glad to have her on the mission. For her, failure would not be an option.

"Are you ready?" she asked.

"Yeah," he said, taking a deep breath and wiping the sweat of his palms against his pants leg. He figured the good thing about time traveling in the recent past was that he would easily blend in. "I'm ready."

The door opened, and Emilee stepped in. Zac followed, Wand at his side. Standing in the middle of the pentagon, Emilee squared her shoulders and stared straight ahead at the concrete wall opposite her. She held her Wand at stomach level and closed her eyes.

"On the count of three," she said. Zac placed his thumb on top of the device. "One... two... three!"

He pressed down hard, and the familiar sensations came flooding to him like a turbulent storm. Zac felt like he was almost unconscious, his body being tossed back and forth in violent river rapids. He thought someone or something had slammed against his shoulder, and then he could feel the world spinning back into existence.

He opened his eyes. Blurry scenery filled his vision as realized he was on the ground.

"Nice landing," a voice said. It was Emilee's. A hand came toward his face, and he reached out to grab it. She hoisted him to his feet. Her skin felt so soft, and he could feel his heart flutter for a split second.

"Thanks," he said. He looked around. No one had seen him; he was in the middle of a field. "Where are we?"

"I had Chen drop us off a bit further from the site," she said, starting to walk toward the edge of the tree line. "So no one would see our sudden appearance and freak out."

"Has that happened yet?" Zac asked, jogging to catch up to her. He didn't catch his bearings as easily as she did, obviously.

"Not that I know of," she said. "Though I always wonder if anyone's seen us and just thought it was their eyes playing tricks on them or something."

They approached the edge of the clearing and stepped deeper into the wooded area. It was thick and dense, shutting out the light of the sun. About a hundred feet ahead, Zac could see a road that wound its way through the trees.

"Are we there yet?" he asked.

Emilee let out a small laugh. "You sound like my little brother," she said. "It's just down the road. We'll follow it to the site where she was abducted."

Zac caught up to her and walked by her side, now on the road. He could see a playground just ahead.

"I didn't know you had a little brother," he said. "How old is he?"

"Up there," Emilee said, pointing to a small playground. It was as if she hadn't heard what Zac said. "Part of the campground. According to the reports, this is where it happened."

"In the middle of a campground?" Zac said. He slowed his pace to match hers.

"The mom said she went into the shower room and left her daughter playing on the playground. Said she wasn't gone for more than a few minutes, and when she came out, she couldn't find the girl."

"So what do we do?"

"We wait," Emilee said. "The girl is about six years old, brown hair and green eyes. We just need to keep an eye out for her. If we see anything, we memorize what happens and write it down as soon as we get back. We call in a tip to the authorities, and they take it from there."

"And it works?" Zac asked.

"Yeah," Emilee said, watching the playground. "Haven't you ever wondered why Amber Alerts for kidnappings don't last that long? Can't change the past, but we can affect the future. It's the next-best thing."

There was no sign of the girl at the playground. Instead, it was empty except for a lone blue car parked near the shower rooms.

"That's probably the kidnapper's car," Zac said.

"I think so, too. They're probably out here somewhere, waiting for whoever comes by. I think we need to find a place to hide ourselves so we can get a good look at him."

"You assume it's a guy."

"In most cases, it is," Emilee said. "Some pervert or something. Someone who deserves to be locked in jail and have the key thrown into a river." She started crossing the road, trying to get closer, when a white van almost hit her.

"Look out!" Zac yelled. Emilee stepped to the side just in time as the van continued down the road, past the playground toward the campsites.

"Jerk!" she yelled.

They moved to the back of the building, trying to find a place to conceal themselves.

"What if this doesn't work?" Zac asked.

"It will," Emilee said. She brushed a strand of hair from her face and stared at the blue car. "Where are you?" she asked the invisible kidnapper. Still no sign of the girl or of the abductor.

A woman came out of the shower rooms. She stopped when she got to the blue car and looked inside, then spun around and ran toward the playground. "Jessica?!" she yelled.

Emilee and Zac exchanged glances. What was going on?

"Jessica? Where are you?" She began pacing back and forth, looking under every structure of the playground.

"Did we miss it?" Zac asked.

Emilee shook her head. "I don't think so," she said. "Unless…"

The woman spotted them, and came running over. Panic filled her eyes. "Help me, please!" She grabbed Zac by the arm. "I can't find my daughter. I left her here for just a few minutes. She might have wandered off, but I told her to stay put!" She called out again. "Jessica!"

It didn't make sense, Zac thought. There was nobody here. They didn't see the little girl playing, not a soul. Only a white van that almost hit Emilee because it was driving so fast—

The van.

Zac turned to Emilee. "We're too late!"

"What?"

"The van. It didn't have any windows. I think we just missed the kidnapping by a minute or two somehow, and the van turned around to make it look like they were coming down the road instead of leaving, trying to cover their tracks."

Emilee stood, a sudden dread coming over her as she considered the possibility. "Did you get a good enough look to give a description?" she asked.

"I think so," Zac said, nodding. He looked down the road. The van was back, this time leaving the campsites, down the road and out of the park. "Look!"

Emilee turned. "That's the one. We just need to get the license plate. We can't miss this opportunity."

The van came closer, and Zac could see a bald man inside it. The man cast a quick glance at Zac, and with what seemed to be a knowing look, sped up.

Zac took off running after it.

"Zac!" Emilee tried running after him, but Zac's legs moved faster as a burst of adrenaline propelled him forward. He couldn't stand there helpless while some little girl was terrified out of her mind, probably tied up in the back. He raced after it, coming to a bend in the road.

The van slowed down to navigate the curve, and Zac gained on it. He reached out to grab the back door handles, his fingers brushing against one but not grabbing it.

He cursed and ran forward, arms and legs pumping like he had never experienced. He had to do more than just get a license plate number.

He had to get the little girl.

He gritted his teeth as he bolted forward, and his chest burned as his lungs expanded with each breath of air. His heart felt like it would burst from his chest any second, and his feet slammed down hard onto the pavement with each step.

The van was picking up speed. He knew he had only been after it for a few seconds, but it felt like forever. He was losing strength and could feel his pace slowing down. He couldn't catch up to it. Not unless something happened that made the van slow down again.

As the van continued to drive out of sight, he made a last effort to get the numbers, straining to see them.

He stopped running. His legs gave way, dropping him to the ground. He tried catching his breath.

He was so close. He had felt the metal of the door handle with his fingertips; if he had only been a little bit faster. If he had only started after it a second or two earlier, he might have been able to do something more.

Just a few seconds. That was all he needed. He was able to travel back in time to try to save this girl, and yet it all came down to a few seconds.

Emilee came running up behind him. "Are you insane? What were you thinking?" she yelled.

"I almost had it," Zac said.

"Zac, you could have been hurt," she said. "And you could have put the girl in worse danger, too!" She looked around, scanning the woods. They were too late.

"I have an idea," Zac said. "We can just do it again."

"What?"

"You know... we can travel in time. Why can't we just come back again? Just a little earlier?"

Emilee shook her head. "It's too risky," she said.

"How?"

"We could run into ourselves. The 'us' that's here now. It could mess things up even worse. Time travel is not something you can just play with. There are serious consequences to consider."

Zac stood up, panting, and brushed himself off. "So this was it?"

Emilee nodded. "We only have one chance. We can't risk a second. We just have to go back with whatever information we have."

Zac took a deep breath and exhaled, his heart rate slowing down. He smiled. "Good thing I got the license plate number."

TWELVE

The underground room was empty when they arrived back. Without thinking, Zac stepped out of the glass doors and hurried to the journal, furiously scribbling down any information he could remember from the encounter. Breathing hard, he handed it to Emilee and wiped the sweat from his forehead.

"Here," he said. "Take it."

Emilee combed over the notes, eyes wide. "You got all that?"

Zac looked up, furrowing his brow. "What do you mean?"

"This… detail," she said. "You caught an amazing amount of information. How did you do that? You were running so fast after the van, I didn't think you would catch anything at all."

He shrugged. "I don't know. It was easy. I've always been good at remembering things."

Emilee shook her head in amazement, her eyes never leaving the paper. "I'll say." She looked up at him. It was one of the first times he'd seen her eyes in a long time. They were honest and open. "I think you've found your calling here."

Zac blushed.

Emilee turned up the hallway and began jogging. "I'm going to go turn this in. Hopefully they can get this scumbag before he does anything stupid."

Zac took a deep breath and leaned against the wall. It felt great to be taking action for once, to not simply be sitting on the sidelines. He felt a sense of purpose, like he had found his place in life. Only he wouldn't be able to tell anyone about it.

He thought about how difficult it would be to balance this and school. But it was only for another year and a half; then he could devote himself full time to it. Even so, he craved the rush he felt; he longed to stand on the platform and use the wormhole again.

He looked down at the Wand in his hand. He had no idea why it worked for him like it did, but he was just glad *that* it did. If he hadn't accidentally found it, and it hadn't malfunctioned, he probably would have told his dad about the underground room. His dad would have been able to make something up about it, and Zac would have never known the truth.

But that wasn't the case. The Wand activated, the wormhole drew him in, and he went back to the day he was born. His mind whirled with the possibilities, the things he could see. All of the events he'd read about in history, the famous speeches, battles, discoveries... they were all waiting for him. All he had to do was use the Wand, and he would be there.

He thought it was funny that they had decided to call the device a Wand. The letters all stood for something: Wormhole Activation Network Device. But it was like a magic wand with all of the capabilities it gave the user.

He heard footsteps and turned to see who was coming down the hallway. Chen approached, carrying a bunch of electronic parts.

"Glad you're back," he said. "Did you run into any Morlocks?"

"Huh?"

"Just joking. It's from the book *The Time Machine*. Where's Emilee?"

"She's calling the information in. I hope it's enough."

"It probably is." Chen slid against the wall and sat down on the floor. "So tell me about it. Was it easy?"

Zac told him everything, how he almost caught up to the van and how they missed the actual abduction. "Hey, let me ask you a question," he said. "Emilee said something about not being able to go back to the time of the incident because we might run into ourselves again. Is that true? We only get one chance?"

Chen nodded. "Yeah, it's a precaution we take. Not that we *couldn't* go back again if we'd wanted to. It's certainly possible. It's just not a good idea."

"I still don't see why not," Zac said, sitting down with his back against the glass door to the wormhole platform. "If we're careful, things should be fine."

"Not really," Chen said, shaking his head. "There are too many things that could backfire on you. There are so many variables to time travel that you can't just have 'do-overs.'"

"But can you really mess something up by observing it again? Even if you're careful?"

"Possibly," Chen said. "Ray Bradbury wrote about this in his story called 'A Sound of Thunder.' In it, a company travels to the past for tourists, but they're careful, because even if someone crushes a bug, they think it'll have time-altering consequences."

"Do you think that's true?"

He waved his hand. "I don't think so. I think we'd have seen the effects by now. But there's no real way to be sure."

Emilee came back down the stairs. "Okay. Called it in. Now we just wait." She stretched. "I don't know about you guys, but I'm starving. Anyone want to get a bite to eat?"

"Sounds good to me," Chen said.

"Sure," Zac said. "I could go." Maybe with someone else around, Emilee would open up a bit more. As long as Rock wasn't around. He wasn't a bad guy or anything; Zac just felt a little bit uneasy around him. It was clear that Rock liked Emilee more than just as a friend. And unfortunately for Zac, she liked him, too.

When they arrived at the restaurant, Bryce and Rock were sitting at a table, waiting for them. They put an extra table next to theirs and pulled up some chairs.

"What's up?" Rock asked. "How'd it go?"

"Could have been better," Zac said. "But I think we gave the authorities something good to go on."

"Good," Bryce said. "That's all you can do."

The waitress came over and took their orders. The room was loud, and it was difficult to hear each other over the sports playing on the televisions in the bar.

"So how do you guys do it?" Zac asked. "How do you go about your daily life and go to class and everything, knowing that you can't tell people what you do at TEMPUS?"

"It's tough," Bryce said. "I'd love to tell people, but obviously we can't."

"Our victories are silent," Chen said. "We get the satisfaction of knowing we did something great, but we can never tell anyone."

Rock nodded. "Think about it: if we told the world that we had the ability to time travel, how do you think they'd respond?" He didn't wait for an answer. "Everyone would be lined up at our door, asking us to fix something from their past, or they'd want to do it themselves. They'd mess everything up. How selfish is *that?*"

Zac squirmed a little in his seat. "I wouldn't call it selfish," he said. "If you could bring back your brother, wouldn't you want to try?"

The table grew silent. Everyone exchanged nervous glances. "Who told you about that?"

Zac looked at the others at the table as if asking for help answering. When no help came, he finally said, "Um, my dad told me. He didn't say much; he just said that something went wrong and he was to blame."

Rock softened and the tension in the room lessened. "Nah, it wasn't his fault. It's just what happened. I don't blame the Doc. But as much as I miss my brother, I still wouldn't go back and change it. I grew a lot from it. Yeah, it was rough at first. But it brought my whole family together. Before that, we never talked."

Zac hadn't thought about the good that could come from the sadness. He couldn't think of how his mom's death had made him stronger. If nothing else, it caused a rift between him and his dad at first. His dad spent all of his spare time working, and now Zac had an inkling of what that work was all about.

He had an idea. He might not be allowed to go back and save his mom, but that didn't mean he couldn't go back and at least *see* her one more time. He'd have to figure out how to gain access to the computer that set the wormhole coordinates. One of them had to know.

"So," said Chen, "if you could change one thing, what would it be? Either in your life or something else about the world's history?"

"I don't know," Zac lied. "I'll pass. What about you?"

"Me? I'd love to go back and tell my dad what companies to invest in. Microsoft... buy a few shares from Bill Gates..."

"Not how you'd use your present knowledge to manipulate things," Bryce said. "If you could fix something, what would it be?"

"Okay, then," Chen said. "What about you?"

Bryce was quiet for a moment. He stared down at his soda, his finger tracing the rim of the glass. "My mom," he said. "I know it's impossible to fix what happened to her, but I would give anything for another chance to see her one more time. Of course, I'd love to tell her to stay home that day, to not leave her apartment..."

Rock patted him on the shoulder. "I told you it shouldn't have been you to go into the training again," he said. "You can't keep doing this to yourself, man."

Chen sensed the awkwardness and tried to change the subject. "What about you, Emilee?"

She looked like a deer caught in the headlights. Zac knew why, but he wondered who else she'd told about her past. "I don't know," she started, but was quickly cut off by cheering coming from the bar.

Everyone was gathered around the televisions, watching the news story that had broken in.

"What's going on?" Bryce asked a man.

"They found her," a waiter said. "That little girl that disappeared."

Zac felt a chill run up his spine. "They... how?" he asked.

"News anchor says someone called in a tip. They traced the plates back to the kidnapper's place and found her. They're taking him in for questioning now."

As Zac stood in stunned silence, paralyzed and in shock from the good news, Bryce put his hand on Zac's shoulder.

"See?" he said. "It's worth it. That's all you, man."

Zac smiled to himself. He wanted to shout out that *he* was the one who'd turned the kidnapper in, that *he'd* been the witness.

He was proud of it, but he knew he couldn't say anything. A feeling of pride swelled over him. "I'm buying dessert," he told the others at the table. He looked over at Emilee, who caught his glance and gave a quick smile.

They had done it. And Zac knew that when the moment arrived, he'd jump onto the platform again, ready to take on whatever the space-time continuum would throw at him. Nothing could stop him now.

Zac walked through the door to his house, and his dad was sitting on the couch watching a movie, waiting for him.

"Nice work," he said. "I didn't get to talk to you before you guys went out. So how's it feel?"

"I think I'm still in a bit of shock," he said, plopping himself down on the sofa. "So much has happened in the past few days."

His dad got up and put some popcorn in the microwave, turning it on. "I've only been on a few time leaps, but I don't think I'll ever get used to it either." He sighed. "I don't think my body can handle it too much."

Zac sat quietly, staring at the television screen. Finally, he spoke. "Dad, have you ever gone to see her?"

"Who?"

"You know who, Dad. Have you gone to see Mom?"

The microwave beeped, and he took the popcorn out, shaking the bag. "Of course," he said, opening the bag and letting the steam pour out. "I went to her grave the other day and visited. You may not have realized this, but when I had them build the TEMPUS headquarters, I made sure it was near the cemetery. That way, I could always be near her no matter what. It's just a short distance away." He sat down.

"That's not what I mean," Zac said. "I mean have you *seen* her? Have you used the machine to go back and see her?"

His dad was silent for a while. "Never," he finally said. "I can't."

"Can't, or *won't?*" Zac asked. "Because if I had built this thing, I would at least go see her once. Wouldn't you want to just go look at her or watch her one more time?"

Dr. Ryger set the popcorn down on the couch and turned to face Zac, ignoring the movie. "Son, I haven't tried to see her because I don't need a time machine to do that. I see her every day."

"What? In a picture? It's not the same, Dad."

"No," he said, holding up his hand, "I know it's not, but think about it. What are pictures, but *frozen moments* in time? With that simple technology, we've managed to take a split second and, using the photons of light, capture it forever. That second will never happen again; it is unique in the universe. Yet we're able to hold on to it."

Zac had never thought of it that way. With digital cameras and smart phones, taking pictures was so quick and easy now that it didn't seem like anything special. But his dad was right; it was revolutionary at the time the capability first emerged.

"But the main reason I don't need a time machine," his dad continued, "is because I have those moments of time frozen up *here* as well." He pointed to his head. "Your mom lives in my memories. In yours. Time's just a series of memories. Some of them can stay with us, seeming like they'll never end. Others are forgotten. But those memories are things we can go to any time we want. It's not limited by technology."

"That's still not the same," Zac said, reaching over and grabbing some popcorn.

"True," he acknowledged. "But Einstein talked about time being relative, and I think this is what he meant. I can remember a specific moment with your mom, and it can stay with me all day if I want it to, even if the actual event only took a few minutes. And of course, there are other times that last a bit *too* long in my memory."

Zac knew what he was referring to, and he didn't want to think about it. "So is that why you don't have the date of her death on the grave marker?" he asked. "Because you think you'd be too tempted to try and go back and stop her killer?" He'd never considered that maybe his dad faced the same temptation he did.

"No, Son. I can never forget that day, the way she was shot in front of all those people. All I remember was a man coming at *you*, trying to get you to come with him. I tried to stop him, and there was a struggle. Someone else tried to help us, trying to wrestle the gun away, and then your mother was shot. It was all such a blur. I just remember being so full of rage that I attacked the person who shot her, though I have no clue what he looked like or how he got away."

"Then why isn't the day she died on the grave marker?" Zac asked.

"It was," his dad said. "But once I built the machine, I realized I'd have to get rid of the date."

"That doesn't make sense."

"Zac, I didn't have it removed so that I couldn't change things. I had it removed in case *you* ever found out about what I did, and so *you'd* never be able to go back and try to save her."

Zac didn't sleep much that night. He had homework to catch up on, and he realized just how hard it was going to be trying to lead a double life. He felt like Spider-Man, attending class during the day but having his "other" life constantly hanging over his head.

He almost fell asleep in class a few times, dozing with his head falling forward, propped up by his hand. In one class, he was slipping into a dream when he heard, "Wake up! Someone wake him up!" His economics teacher berated him in front of the class, but he didn't care. Tomorrow was Saturday, and he could sleep in.

Arriving at the TEMPUS headquarters that evening, he found that there was nothing new for him to do. On the one hand, he was glad to have nothing new, because that meant there was no crime, but deep down, he craved the adventure. If he couldn't prevent a crime, maybe he could go on an observation mission, one in which he used the machine to learn about things that had already happened.

Zac approached his dad with the idea while he was sitting in his office. "Isn't that the reason you built TEMPUS? To observe without interfering? The machine can be used so that we know what *really* happened in the past, not just what textbooks say. So how about it? Can you send me?"

At first hesitant, his dad mulled the suggestion over. "Maybe," he said. "What did you have in mind?"

Zac smiled. "Roswell."

Dr. Ryger raised his eyebrows. "New Mexico? The rumored spaceship crash?" He stood up and walked over to his file cabinet, putting some documents in manila folders. "I don't think so. That's not like going back to just a day or two ago. It's a whole different time period. You're talking 1947; you haven't been on enough missions to go on an observation like that." He shook his head. "Sorry. It was hard enough for me to let you assist Emilee on the last one, to even let you be involved with TEMPUS. I'm not ready to let you go on something like that."

"Oh, come on," Zac pleaded. "I read up on it. It happened during a lightning storm in the middle of a ranch, *miles* away from where people lived. All we would have to do is get there, observe the crash, and get back before anyone would see us. It's the perfect observation mission. No one would see us arrive, and no one would see us leave."

His dad looked out the window into the distance. "I don't know," he said. "I still think it's too risky."

"I won't be alone," Zac said. "We can take more than two people, right? So let the others come with me." He walked over to the window, grabbing his dad by the forearm and making him turn to look him in the eye. "I know you're worried about me wanting to change the past with Mom, but I need you to trust me. I'll be careful. What better use for this machine than to put to rest some conspiracy theories? If it's a weather balloon, like some people say, we'll know. And if it's not, we can finally know that we're not alone in the universe."

His dad sighed. "Maybe. Let me consult with the rest of the team. If enough of them want to go, then it might be an okay idea. I've been wanting to use the technology to get a more accurate picture of historical events; maybe this *is* the perfect first step. A barren field, no one around... let me think about it."

"Awesome," Zac said, and left. As he got into his car, he thought about how remarkable it would be to witness the most famous "flying saucer" event in United States history. Of course, it could always just be a weather balloon.

But what if it wasn't? What if *he* was the first person to welcome these extraterrestrials to Earth?

THIRTEEN

"Wake up."

A voice broke into Zac's sleep, mixing with his dream until he realized it was coming from someone in his room. He sat up and turned to see his dad standing in the doorway.

"What time is it?"

"It's time to go," his dad said. "I'm going to let you do the leap to Roswell. But Bryce and Emilee are going with you; I've already spoken to them."

Zac bolted up. "Seriously? We can do it?"

"Yeah. I figure with three people, it's safe enough to go. I'm still a little uneasy about it, but Bryce is the best there is at this. He's been on more time leaps than any one of us. I figure if any problems come up, he'll be able to handle them." He started down the hallway. "Get ready. We'll head over together."

Zac got dressed in a hurry, throwing on some blue jeans and a black long-sleeve shirt. The leap would take him to the middle of a

99

ranch, but if it was in the middle of the night, it could be cold. Black would be best so that he would be even less noticeable. He didn't think anyone would see him, but it couldn't hurt to be extra careful.

He grabbed a bagel and shoved it into his mouth, barely taking the time to chew before he swallowed. He almost choked and washed it down with some soda. He knew he'd need the caffeine although he slept pretty well last night.

He couldn't believe his dad was going to let him do this. But then again, his dad was always devoted to his work; even before Zac knew about the TEMPUS project and what his dad was really doing, he watched as his dad worked night and day on it. Zac sometimes felt like he didn't exist, and resentment set in.

Now that he knew it was because his dad was working with *time travel*, it was a little easier for him to understand. But how could his dad spend so much time working on the machine without trying to find a way to save his mom? He was starting to accept that his dad couldn't alter history. But what if the changes that bled down were actually for the better? Of course, there was no real way to know the effects, but deep down, Zac thought that there had to be a way to both save his mom and still be careful enough that it wouldn't have a huge effect on altering time.

Then again, maybe his dad *had* tried to figure it all out already. Maybe that was why he was always working, devoted to finding a way to make it happen. Maybe Zac would see something his dad had missed. He could look at it from a different perspective. Even though everyone said it was impossible, he still had hope.

Zac brimmed with excitement and anticipation as he sat in the passenger seat of the car. His dad was talking about all of the different events he wanted to have the team go back and witness someday if this leap was a success. Maybe once the world was ready, it would be possible to rewrite the history books, this time with complete confidence that what was written was based on eyewitnesses and was the complete truth.

They drove past the school, about half a mile away from TEMPUS. Zac looked at the marker that was placed next to where the time capsule was buried. He could see that the dirt was still freshly disturbed from where they had filled in the hole.

"So Dad," he said, looking at the marker, "what did you have me put in the time capsule? What was in the envelope?"

His dad didn't answer, but shifted in his seat uncomfortably.

"Was it about time travel? About the machine?" Zac asked.

"Not exactly. It's hard to explain. It's just something I wrote for the people who open it two hundred years from now. They won't need the plans for TEMPUS; their technology will be so much more advanced than our own by then. Think about how far we've come in the past two centuries."

"Then what could possibly be so important that you had me put in the time capsule?"

The car turned into the parking lot of the office building where the TEMPUS headquarters were housed. "I just wrote about the most important discovery I've made through my work. Something I want to be remembered for."

The pentagon was glowing a vibrant blue when Zac descended the hallway with his dad. Emilee and Bryce were standing next to it, waiting. In their hands they each held a Wand.

"You ready for this?" Bryce asked, handing Zac his Wand.

"Yeah, I think so," Zac answered. "You?"

Bryce waved it off. "Piece of cake. It's just an in and out time leap. Chen is going to get us as close to the estimated time of the crash as possible." He began walking down the hallway to the control area where Chen stood, typing furiously at the computer. "Everything going okay?"

"Yep," Chen said, eyes fixed on the screen. "I've tried to calculate the best time to have the wormhole open up for you, but of course, it could be a bit off."

Emilee came around the corner and walked over to the computer. "Let me check it for a second." She scanned the screen full of parameters, letters and numbers that Zac couldn't make sense of.

"How do you understand all of that?" Zac asked. "It looks like nonsense to me."

"It's easy for me," Emilee said, "because I helped design the program." She finished entering some data into the computer and stepped back, giving the screen one last look. "Your dad took care of the scientific stuff and I wrote the program that operates it."

"Uh, hello?" Bryce said, pointing to himself.

"Okay," Emilee said, smiling slightly, "Bryce helped a little. So we pretty much know how it all works." She pointed to the screen. "I just made sure that the program would be able to direct the wormhole to open up in an area of calm weather if the lightning storm was happening. It might deposit us a bit farther away, but hopefully not too much. It's just a safety precaution." She walked back toward the platform.

Bryce and Zac followed. "Wait—what happens if lightning hits the wormhole?" Zac asked.

"Shouldn't be an issue," Bryce told him. "It should work just like normal. In theory, lightning would just discharge energy into the wormhole, which requires a lot of energy anyway."

"So it's ready?" Zac asked.

"You're good to go," Chen said. "The Wands are powered up and ready. I'll be here to monitor the machine. Just keep an eye on the Wands' indicator lights. I don't know how close to the time of the crash it will place you, so if you're waiting a while, it might be better to come back so your Wands don't run out of power."

"Thanks," Bryce said. They approached the platform and the glass doors opened. Emilee stepped into the chamber first, followed by Bryce and Zac.

Zac's dad stood watching, his arms crossed. He rose up and down on the balls of his feet in nervousness. Zac could see the concern in his eyes, but it was mixed with excitement and anticipation. Zac nodded to him, an understanding that things would be fine.

The sound of hurried footsteps echoed from the hallway. Before the door was able to close, Rock came bounding into the room.

"Whoa, whoa! I'm not going to let you guys do this without me!" He reached over for his Wand in the case on the wall, pushing past Zac's dad. "Sorry, Doc. I didn't get your message until just a few minutes ago." He yelled around the corner. "Hey, Chen! Hold up a second!" He stepped into the chamber between Emilee and Zac. "Okay, ready!"

The door closed, and a loud humming began to vibrate through the concrete room. Zac had gotten used to it, but the reverberations still sounded like a jackhammer in his ears. The blue light beneath his feet grew brighter, and he could almost feel the shaking sensation beginning.

"On three," Bryce said, raising the Wand. The others followed suit.

Zac gripped his tightly.

"One… two… thr—,"

Zac pressed hard, and he felt like his body was being tossed around. It was almost like being in a roller coaster ride full of twists and turns, thrashing his body back and forth. His head felt like it was being slammed against the headrest, and it felt like his breath was being sucked from his lungs. His chest felt a crushing weight on it, and then he felt a sharp pain in his back.

The movement stopped, and he opened his eyes. An eerie silence engulfed him as he gazed at the night sky. It looked as if the stars above him were rotating, and he sat up, still dizzy. He closed his eyes and steadied himself.

Zac stood up. "Hello?" he said out loud. "Bryce?" He turned around, looking for the rest of the team. It was so dark out that he could barely see a thing. The only light came from the moon and whatever reflected its light. His eyes adjusted to the dim light, and he could slowly make out the shape of the land, flat in the distance as far as he could see. To one side, it looked like a forest, the trees reaching up toward the sky.

"Zac?" It was Emilee. "Where are you?" He could hear her footsteps coming closer.

"Over here." Zac moved toward her voice, and they met. "Where are Bryce and Rock?"

"I don't know. Usually when we leap together, we all land in the same spot. For some reason, we're farther away than usual."

Zac scanned the horizon. Now he was starting to see more, the moon's light bathing everything in a wash of whites and grays. It almost looked like the wormhole had dumped them off into an old black and white movie.

"There!" she said, pointing. In the distance, Zac could make out two dark silhouettes coming toward them. "Good, they made it." She started walking toward the shapes, and Zac followed.

"That was wild," Rock said as they got closer. "You guys okay?"

"Yeah," Zac said. "My back hurts. I think I landed on a rock or something."

"At least we avoided the lightning storm," Bryce said. "Any idea where we are?"

The team looked around, unfamiliar with their surroundings.

"Maybe landing in the middle of nowhere wasn't such a great idea after all," Zac said.

"It'll be fine," Bryce said. "We just need to watch the skies for the lightning storm. If we see something strange, we might be able to determine if it's the crash or not."

"So what do you want to do, Bryce? You're the unofficial leader," Rock said.

Bryce surveyed the area. "I think we should try to find a high point that we can watch from and use as shelter during the storm."

"Sounds good to me," Rock said. "See anything?"

Bryce shook his head. "No. Looks like a forest or something that way," he said, pointing at the growth of trees. "I say we head in the other direction a bit. It looks like the land rises up into a rocky outcropping that way. Maybe there's something over there."

They agreed and started walking. The night was quiet except for the noise of the insects and a few other animals calling to each other. Even though Zac was familiar with the sounds, something seemed different. He couldn't quite place his finger on it. Nervously, he looked around.

He glanced up to see the moon. The sky was so much clearer out here, and even with the cloud cover, the moon and the stars were so much more vibrant. In the city, it was easy to forget that so many celestial bodies filled the night sky.

As he looked, a dark shape like a massive shadow flew past the moon, temporarily blocking its light.

"What was that?" Emilee asked.

"I don't know," Bryce said. "Probably some kind of bird. A hawk or something."

"That didn't look like any hawk I've ever seen," Rock said. "It was big."

They could see the rocks about five hundred feet ahead of them. The top surface looked flat enough that they could rest on it and watch, and there seemed to be another thin rock jutting out at an angle just to the right of it. Perfect to use as shelter if they needed it.

Zac looked back toward the tree line in the distance. He could see tiny glowing spots, yellow and reflective. Some kind of animal was watching them. And it looked like there was more than one.

"You guys see that back there?" Zac asked. Everyone stopped and turned. "What do you think that is?"

Bryce took a step closer. "Some animals, probably. It's hard to tell from this far away. Just a group of them."

"Yeah, I guess," Zac said. "It's just creepy. It's like they're watching us."

"I wouldn't worry about it," Bryce said. "There are lots of animals on a huge ranch like this one."

"As long as they're not wolves," Rock said. "Aren't they on ranches, too?"

"Those look too big to be wolves," Zac said. "Look." The shapes were stirring as if they were moving, the eyes looking back and forth among themselves. Zac stared, trying to get a better look at the shapes. "It looks like they're on two legs. Look how they're moving."

"I don't like this," Rock said after a moment's hesitation. He looked at Emilee. "None of this is freaking you out?"

Emilee turned away from the shapes. They were still far away, but it looked like they were moving in the team's direction. "Come on," she said, pointing. "Let's get to the high ground. Whatever animals those are, they won't be able to climb up something that steep."

Zac gave the shapes one last look and started moving again, this time at a much quicker pace.

A few minutes later, they arrived at the base of the rock structure. It looked like something had caused a landslide, and the side resembled a small cliff about twenty feet up.

"Ladies first," Bryce said. Emilee turned and glared, then placed her hand on a rock that stuck out from the side. She was strong and muscular, and she scaled the side with ease, moving up it like a spider as she found handholds and footholds along the way. She reached the top and disappeared over the edge.

"So?" yelled Bryce loud enough for her to hear him. "Is it okay for us to come up?"

"Yeah," she shouted back, looking over the side. "It's fine up here."

"You wanna go next?" Bryce asked, gesturing to the base of the rocks.

"You go ahead," Zac said. "I'm not such a good climber. I'd just slow us down."

Bryce grabbed ahold of the rock and began pulling himself up, strategically placing his feet in places to give him the best footing. When he was about halfway up, Zac turned to Rock. "Your turn."

"No, you go ahead," Rock said. "I'll go last. I don't care for heights, so I'm not in any hurry."

"Okay," Zac said. He looked up to see the silhouette of Bryce roll over the side and out of sight. He had made it to the top.

Zac placed his hand on the rock and gripped it, making sure he could hold on. His fingers wrapped around the top of the handhold, and he could feel the dirt in his fingernails. Something crawled across his hand and he jerked it back, then found another place to grab. He lifted his foot, pushing down to try to find a place that would support his weight. He felt his foot make contact, and pressed down to make sure he could use it to push up to the next level.

He continued climbing that way, and when he was about halfway up, Emilee appeared at the rim of the top. "Um, guys," she said, looking behind them into the distance. Bryce joined her, gazing intently. "I don't want to worry you, but those animals we were talking about earlier? They're getting closer. And fast. You'd better hurry up."

As Zac grabbed his next handhold, he heard Bryce say to Emilee, "Are you seeing what I'm seeing? Are those…" But then his voice dropped off.

"I hope not," Emilee said. "Because if that's true, then we've got bigger problems than just climbing up to this ledge."

FOURTEEN

Zac's heart quickened, and he tried to climb faster. Rock started behind him, and Zac was careful not to let his feet break away any rock or dirt that would fall down on him.

What did Emilee see? What was she so worried about? Bryce himself said there was nothing to be concerned about.

"Guys, hurry," Emilee said. "I think something's wrong here. You need to get up here *fast*. Those aren't wolves. I don't think we're in Roswell, at least not the year 1947. I think someone screwed up the time parameters."

"What are they?" Zac shouted up. He wanted to look back, but he was afraid he'd slip.

He could see Emilee's face now, trained on the creatures in the distance. Her gaze was unmoving, but he could see fear in her eyes.

"Just get up here," Bryce said. "Don't stop and don't look back."

Of course, Zac looked back. Immediately he wished he hadn't. He stopped, not believing what he saw.

Moving with stealth across the field behind him were several creatures that walked on their two hind legs. Their movements were quick and jerky, their heads darting back and forth. As they got closer, he could see their skin reflecting the moonlight, pebbly and rough. It was almost… reptilian.

"Keep moving," Rock said from behind him. He was calm, but he hadn't looked back yet. "I'm right at your feet."

Zac turned back to the task in front of him. His palms were sweaty now, and as he lifted his right foot to step on the next foothold, he felt something slip out of his pocket.

"What was that?" Rock asked, looking down as the object fell past him.

Zac's eyes grew wide. "The Wand! It fell out of my pocket!"

Bryce yelled from above. "What did you say?"

"My Wand! I dropped it!"

"I'll get it," Rock shouted, and began climbing down.

"No, Rock! You can't do that!" Emilee yelled. "They're right there!"

But Rock couldn't hear them; the wind was blowing hard now. A storm rumbled in the distance.

Zac heard strange, growling noises approaching the base down below. He scrambled to the top of the ledge and hoisted himself over. Quickly, he turned on his stomach and looked down.

Rock was staring out at the field, bending down to reach the Wand. He moved slowly, his back to the wall. He was trapped. He picked up Zac's Wand and put it in his pocket with his own.

And then Zac saw them: five creatures that emerged into the patch of moonlight right in front of Rock. They circled him, stalking him. Zac held his breath; he wanted to yell, but couldn't. Rock was going to die, and it was his fault. Just like it was his dad's fault that Rock's brother had died.

"What do we do?" Emilee asked, panic filling her voice. "They're going to kill him!"

Zac just stared in shock. Unless his eyes were seeing things, the creatures surrounding Rock below were ancient, extinct. He was looking at a pack of dinosaurs. But that couldn't be possible. Dinosaurs didn't exist in 1947. Then that would mean that Emilee was right. The machine had somehow taken them back much further.

He could see them more clearly now. The dinosaurs were about as high as Rock's chest, with a long neck and a small head. They stood on two legs, continually shifting back and forth on them as if nervous or in anticipation of something. Their tails stood straight out from their bodies, balancing them as they moved.

Even from that far up, Zac could smell death on them; rotting meat hung in the air from their breath. The odor was so pungent he wanted to throw up. One of them hissed, and Rock turned to look at it.

"We have to do something!" Zac said, eyes wide. "How do we get rid of them?"

Bryce looked behind himself, searching. He hurried off, and Emilee stood up.

"Where are you going?" she asked. She was starting to walk toward him, but stopped when she heard Rock yell.

Zac and Emilee ran over to the edge to look down. Rock was completely backed against the wall now, trying to turn and grab onto the side and start climbing. Every time he did, one of the dinosaurs hissed and lunged at him. He dodged or swung at them, narrowly avoiding being bitten.

The creatures had sensed his fear and were gaining confidence, moving in for the kill. Unless the team did something soon, Rock was a goner. The growls were growing in intensity, and one of the dinosaurs let out a screech, high-pitched and horrible. It echoed across the field as another peal of thunder rumbled.

Something large hit one of the dinosaurs on the head, and it looked up with a growl. Bryce was standing at the edge, his arms filled with rocks larger than his fists.

"Take some and start chucking," he said.

Zac and Emilee grabbed what they could and began hurling the stones down at the dinosaurs. Zac missed several times, but one rock came close. Emilee hit one at the base of its tail, but all of their efforts did little to scare away the dinosaurs. It only seemed to anger them.

Finally, Emilee turned to Bryce in desperation. "What else can we do?" Zac had never seen her like this before. Rock was a sitting duck down there, and they all knew it.

And suddenly the thought struck him: he was a sitting duck, too. If there was another way up here, who's to say those things down below wouldn't know a way up? The team would be trapped. What if some were already on their way up?

"Use your Wand!" Emilee yelled. "Just go! Toss Zac's up here and we'll follow after you leave!"

Rock nodded down below and pulled both Wands from his pocket. He dipped low for power, then turned and threw a Wand upward. It missed by a few feet and bounced off the side of the rocks, rolling down to the feet of one of the creatures.

The dinosaur bent low, cocking its head to the side as its glowing eyes inspected the device. It reared its head back, staring at it, then decisively darted its head out and bit down on the device. A bright flash and a stream of sparks shot out, and the creature recoiled.

"Oh, crap!" Bryce said, turning to stare at Zac. "Rock, you gotta go now, man! Use it!"

Rock held his hand up slightly and pressed down on the button.

Nothing happened.

Rock held the device up to his eyes and stared at it, looking at the lights on the indicator. They were all still lit. He pressed down again, but nothing happened. He looked up at the three of them. "It's not worki—"

One of the dinosaurs lunged forward, sinking its teeth into his left arm. He screamed, and the creature started to pull him forward. Rock pulled against it, swinging his right fist and punching the creature in the eye. It let go of him and stood back.

"Oh, no," Bryce said. "I think he mixed the Wands up. I think the one he has now is Zac's. Then that would mean the dinosaur…"

Bryce's words were interrupted by a shout from Rock. "What's with this thing?" he asked, pressing down on the Wand. The nearest dinosaur opened its mouth in a loud hissing noise and lunged again. Rock tried to move out of the way, but a second one moved in and grabbed his leg, yanking him off his feet.

Emilee screamed.

Rock kicked and flailed his arms, but it had no effect. The first creature struck its head in, knocking Zac's Wand from Rock's hand. It surveyed the device with curiosity and bit into it. The bright flash made it open its mouth and shake its head to get rid of the pain.

"Now what do we do?" Zac asked in panic. "Both of our Wands are destroyed! How will we get back?" He was sweating, his hands shaking.

"Stay calm," Bryce ordered, eyes focused below.

The other dinosaurs began moving in on Rock, each fighting the others for their prey.

Rock lay on the ground, his left arm bleeding profusely. His right hand had lacerations, and he was being pulled further away from the base of the rocks as the other dinosaurs moved back, making room for their dinner.

Rock reached for one of the stones Bryce had thrown and grabbed it with his left hand. The dinosaurs stopped dragging him, and one of them approached, this one slightly larger than the others.

The alpha male.

Placing its foot on Rock's chest and pressing down, it stared at him. Opening its mouth, it lunged for his throat. Rock's right hand shot up and grabbed the creature by its neck. With a yell that echoed through the field, he swung his left arm at the creature's head, smashing the stone into its skull. The dinosaur stumbled, falling forward momentarily.

Rock grabbed its head with both hands and, placing his thumbs in its eyes, pushed as hard as he could.

The creature gave an unearthly shriek, the sound a demon might make dragging a soul to the underworld. The rest of the dinosaurs backed off. The alpha male staggered backwards.

At that moment, the air was filled with a sound louder and deeper than thunder. Something else had made the noise. Something living. Zac felt the vibrations rumble through him, and the hair on the back of his neck stood on end.

The dinosaurs that were surrounding Rock seemed agitated by something. One by one, they ran back toward the forest.

The noise rumbled again, and this time it was followed by a low, guttural growl. Zac knew one thing: it wasn't thunder that scared the other dinosaurs off. It was something bigger, something more threatening. And it was coming toward them.

He turned to Bryce and Emilee. "What do we do?" he asked. "Are those Wands broken? They did something to both of them."

"They're gone," Bryce said, staring down at Rock, who was trying to get to his feet. "How in the hell did we end up *here*? We were supposed to go to 1947." He stared straight ahead, unblinking as if lost in thought. "But this is, like, millions of years ago."

Emilee grabbed him by the shoulder. "We can figure that out later. What do we do about *Rock*? How are we going to get him and Zac back without their Wands?"

They could feel slight vibrations in the ground, moving through their feet. Whatever that large creature was that had scared the others away, it was getting closer.

Bryce turned and checked their surroundings. Could something else be close? He looked off into the distance at all angles. "We've got to do *something* soon," he said, pointing. "Look!"

Zac looked in the direction he indicated and saw a massive shape moving toward them. No doubt it heard the commotion and could probably smell blood in the air. It looked to be the size of something like a tyrannosaurus, but bigger. Zac didn't want to find out how much bigger.

"How can I get back without a Wand?" he asked Bryce. "What about him?" He pointed to Rock, who was trying to stand and climb up. "We can't just leave him!"

Bryce shook his head. "I don't know what else to do. We've never accounted for something like this happening."

"Well, we'd better hurry," Emilee said. "I don't feel safe up here anymore." She looked over her shoulder.

Bryce hesitated. "There *is* one thing we could try," he said. "I have no idea if it will work, but I don't see any other options."

"What is it?" Zac asked.

"We take two people back with each Wand." He looked at his; the lights had gone down to two bars. "I can go get Rock and grab onto him. You could take Zac," he said to Emilee. "These things could run out of power before we figure out another solution."

"Wait," Zac said. "What's so risky about doing it that way? Has anyone done it before?"

"No," Bryce said, shaking his head. "But I think if we form a physical bond, it should take both of us since we're both in the system. The computer program will recognize two users coming back and hopefully, it will let us back without the second Wand."

"What's the other possibility?" Emilee asked.

Bryce shrugged. "It could kill us," he said. "But right now, I'd rather die that way than die here being torn to pieces by the dinosaurs that attacked Rock."

"I agree," Emilee said. "Let's do this. How do we get Rock up here?"

Just then, they heard Rock yell from the base of the ledge. "Hey, guys? I don't think I've got much time left." He tried climbing again, struggling to pull himself up with his injured arms. He slipped and fell down.

The shape of the dinosaur was moving closer. Rock wouldn't make it.

"I'm going after him," Bryce said. "You guys go."

Emilee shook her head. "I'm not leaving until I know you and Rock are safe."

"Suit yourself," Bryce said, and threw his legs over the side. He moved quickly down, often slipping and losing his foothold. Zac watched as he hit the ground and rushed over to Rock, hoisting him up and putting his arm around him for support.

The dinosaur was within a hundred feet of them now. It stopped, surveying its prey. Its leathery skin was covered in scars from forgotten battles, its legs as thick as trees. Two tiny forearms hung in front of it as it bent lower. The teeth were the most terrifying part of it. Each tooth had to be at least the size of Zac's forearm. One bite from this thing and Bryce and Rock would be crushed in half. He prayed that the wormhole would be faster than the dinosaur's jaws.

"Go!" Emilee yelled.

Bryce looked up at them. The tyrannosaur gave an earth-shattering bellow and began charging. Bryce held tightly onto Rock, then pressed his thumb down onto the Wand.

The tyrannosaur opened its mouth and lunged forward, turning its head sideways to grab its meal. It slammed its head into the base of the rock and stumbled back, dazed. The air around it shimmered and undulated, and Bryce and Rock were gone without a trace.

"Thank God," Emilee said. "Okay, now we gotta get out of here."

Zac walked away from the ledge, his eyes still on the dinosaur below. A chill ran up his spine as it looked up at him. Its beady eyes seemed to be following him, making him uneasy. "I never thought about what it would look like when we go back," he said. "I guess I always thought a big, glowing wormhole would pop down out of the sky to vacuum us up."

Emilee didn't seem to hear him. "Come on," she said. "Wrap your arms around me."

Zac approached her and reached out his arms, feeling a little uncomfortable. It felt awkward to be wrapping his arms around her, much like a slow dance at prom.

"Hold on tighter," Emilee said. "We don't know if it worked for them or not. This could be it for us."

Zac looked into her eyes as she wrapped her arms around his waist. For a moment, she looked into his, too, and he thought he was looking at her true self, the Emilee that didn't hide behind a mask of drive and determination. There was emotion in there; there was pain. Zac could feel it.

Emilee sensed it, too, and closed her eyes. "Here we go," she said. "I hope to see you on the other side."

She pressed down on the device, and the last thing Zac heard was the roar of the ancient beast.

FIFTEEN

"What happened?" Zac heard as he arrived back at TEMPUS. He was still holding onto Emilee, and she let go of him as soon as she saw Rock stretched out on the ground outside the pentagon. He was surrounded by Zac's dad and Chen; Bryce sat off to the side in a rolling chair, leaning forward and clutching his head. "What happened to him?" Dr. Ryger asked again.

"The wormhole malfunctioned," Bryce said. "It set us down somewhere in prehistoric times."

"What?" Chen asked. "But that's impossible. I entered the coordinates myself!"

Emilee moved to Rock's side and held his bloodied hand. Rock groaned. "Yeah, well, impossible or not, what do you think did *this*? Prairie dogs?" She stroked his arm.

"I just don't get it," Chen said. "I checked the parameters several times. I went through all of the precautions, *everything*. I don't know how it could have gone wrong, Dr. Ryger."

"Well, we'll have to deal with that later. Right now, we need to get him help," he replied.

Rock whispered something, and Emilee bent down to listen. "We have to get him to a hospital," she said. "He said he can't feel his arm where the dinosaur bit him. He said it's numb and feels like it's spreading."

"Okay," Dr. Ryger said. "Let's get him to the main level. But we need a plausible explanation. We obviously can't tell the hospital he time-travelled or survived a dinosaur attack." He lifted Rock up and together they started walking up the incline. Emilee followed.

Chen ran over to help. "I got you," he said, supporting Rock's other side. "I'm so sorry, man. I have no idea how this happened." He continued apologizing as they walked, and his voice soon became a murmur echoing off the walls as they ascended.

Soon, Zac was left alone in the room with only Bryce. He pulled up another rolling chair and moved close to him. "So what happens now?" he asked.

Bryce didn't even look up. "I don't want to think about it," he said.

"Do you think Rock's going to be okay?"

"I have no idea. He's in pretty bad shape now. I don't know about you and Emilee, but when we travelled together like that, it drained a lot more energy from me than I expected."

"Same here," Zac said. He still felt a bit dizzy and almost sick to his stomach.

"And if his arm is going numb like that..."

Zac looked at the pentagon. "He's going to shut it down, isn't he?"

Bryce took a deep breath. "I don't know. Last time something like this happened, when Rock's brother died, he shut it down for a month. But Rock convinced him to keep going. I don't see that happening this time."

Not that it mattered anyway, Zac thought. His Wand was gone, destroyed by the pack of prehistoric beasts. He couldn't use the machine anymore unless his dad had finished making him the other Wand. But even if he did, he probably wouldn't let Zac use it. His "great idea" to observe the past had blown up in his face. And now, Rock might die because of him.

"What do you think happened?" Zac asked. He got up and began pacing the room. "Do you think Chen entered the information in wrong?"

"I don't know," Bryce said, standing up and walking around the corner toward the computer. "Look," he said, pointing to the screen, "everything's right. I checked it earlier, too."

Zac studied the screen. "Could someone have sabotaged it?"

"Sabotaged?"

"Well, yeah, like another scientist or something," he said.

Bryce shook his head. "You've been watching too many movies," he said. "The only other person who has access to that kind of data is Emilee. She helped create the program, and she knows it inside and out. I don't think she sabotaged her own work."

They heard footsteps echo in the corridor, and soon Zac's dad came into the room.

"Dr. Ryger," Bryce said, "was anyone else down here recently?"

"No," Dr. Ryger said, voice solemn. "Just us."

Bryce studied the screen, staring at it as if it would suddenly provide him with answers.

"Dad, is Rock going to be okay?" Zac asked.

His dad shrugged. "I have no idea. The paramedics took him to the hospital, and now I have the task of calling his parents and explaining the situation to them. I have no idea what to say. They don't know about the project, either. All they know is that they've lost one son who had worked with me. I don't want it to become two."

Zac hung his head. "It's my fault," he whispered.

"That doesn't matter," Dr. Ryger said, sighing. "For now, though, I'm going to have to temporarily disband all use of TEMPUS. It's not safe."

Zac's heart sank. He had hoped that by showing that he could use the machine wisely for a good purpose, he would be able to figure out a way to use it to see his mom again. "Maybe it *did* take us to Roswell, but the year was wrong. Was the computer programmed for 1947 A.D.?"

Bryce shook his head. "There is no B.C. and A.D. in time," he said. "Not really. Those are man-made constructs. But I agree with your dad. We need to sit down and go over the code, line by line, and see if we can figure it out."

"But it was just *one* time," Zac protested. "We can still use it for recent events like we did for that kidnapping the other day, can't we?"

"Zac," Dr. Ryger said, "I've made up my mind. It's over. It's just not safe. Something is malfunctioning inside TEMPUS. First, the prototype Wand you found started working even though it hasn't been assigned to you, and now the wormhole opens up nowhere *near* where it was supposed to. I'm sorry, but there's no way I'm letting you or anyone else go back in until it's fixed." He shoved the empty rolling chair across the room in frustration. "If only you hadn't come down here a week ago, we wouldn't be in this mess."

"You don't know that, Dr. Ryger," Bryce said. "By finding the room and accidentally activating the wormhole, Zac might have showed us how vulnerable the system is. Without him, we might not have found the flaws."

"Yes, but now we don't even have the Wand that was malfunctioning. Maybe that was the cause of everything. But now we'll never know." He exhaled heavily. Zac felt hurt; he hadn't meant to cause any problems. It wasn't his fault that he found the place. If they didn't want him to find it, they shouldn't have let him in the building in the first place. It didn't have military-level security, but that didn't mean they couldn't keep people out.

"I'm sorry," Zac said in frustration. "I didn't mean to cause any problems."

"Of course not," his dad said, "but now we're short two Wands that were left in a different time period. At least they're designed to break down over time if they're damaged." He shoved his hands in his pockets and started walking out of the room. "You know, it doesn't matter," he said, his voice filled with anger. "We'll figure it out. I have bigger problems to deal with right now."

As he stormed off, Zac was filled with immense guilt.

"Don't let it bother you," Bryce said after Dr. Ryger was out of earshot. "He'll calm down in the morning. He just needs to vent a little. This project is his whole life."

Zac rolled his eyes. Of course it was, he thought. Work always was. And this just proved it. His dad didn't even ask once how *he* was after this ordeal. He could have been killed by a prehistoric creature or left for dead in the past, but all his dad cared about was the project.

"I guess some things never change," Zac said.

When Zac arrived home that evening, he walked right past his father into the living room. Dr. Ryger sat studying something at his desk in the other room, scribbling something into a notebook. Zac wanted to get a closer look at what he was writing, and he inched closer to try and look over his shoulder. He peered at the black marks that were written with such haste that they looked like nothing but black squiggles.

His dad's hand moved in a blur, then brought the pen down with force onto the notebook and remained still. "What?" Dr. Ryger said without looking up.

"Nothing," Zac said, caught off guard. "I just wondered what you were working on."

"Well if *I'm* working on it, then it's probably not intended for *you* to be looking at, is it?"

Zac backed off and walked back toward the living room. He had hit a nerve and knew better than to keep pressing. Instead, an awkward silence filled the room as he sat down to watch television. He turned it on, flipping through the channels, not really watching anything, but just doing it to be doing something.

"Do you mind turning it down?" his dad asked. It wasn't really a question, and Zac turned it down a little bit.

He wished his dad would just talk to him, yell at him for messing things up. Anything was better than this cold and harsh silence. Hadn't he been punished enough already? It was his fault that no one else would be able to use TEMPUS. His fault that now, other crimes wouldn't be solved and lives could be lost. If it weren't against the rules of time travel, he'd love to be able to go back and tell himself to just shut up, to not even suggest trying to go to Roswell.

The silent treatment grew unbearable, and Zac stormed into the other room. "I know you're upset, but we can't do this. I know we can figure out a way to keep the project from being shut down."

"Zac, you don't understand," his dad said, turning to look at him. "This project isn't just something of mine. I'm just a physicist who runs it and carries out the work. I've solicited and borrowed money from lots of wealthy people, people whose names you'd know in an instant if I told you. I told them of all the good we can do if given the time and technology to develop TEMPUS. And now, they're going to demand answers for why the technology isn't working properly. If they find out about this and get nervous, they're not going to want to invest money in it anymore. They don't want to be slapped with a lawsuit that could cost them everything. They're risk-takers, but some things are too risky."

"Just talk to them," Zac said. "If they know that what you're building is that extraordinary, I'm sure they'll be willing to give you more time to—"

"You don't get it, Zac," he said. "It's not just me. I didn't build TEMPUS all by myself. Do you think I figured out how to create the portal to the wormhole without any help? That took money and technology, more brilliant minds than you'd believe. It's not magic that powers that thing!"

Zac was quiet, contemplating what to say. He knew his dad wasn't going to change his mind about shutting it down, but he had to try. If only he could fix the problem that caused it. An idea came to him.

"Wait," he said. "What about sending someone else back to the site where Rock was attacked by the dinosaurs? Bryce and I can't go, but maybe Chen could. *He* could go to that time and warn us to leave before the attack even occurred, and then you wouldn't have to worry about any of this." He smiled, proud that he had thought of it.

Dr. Ryger shook his head and put his hand up. "Don't you think I've already considered that?" He sighed. "It won't work."

"Why not? We wouldn't be running into ourselves, would we? It would be someone different."

"It doesn't matter. If Chen went back and gave you the warning, Rock wouldn't be injured. But if Rock doesn't come back injured, then Chen won't go back in time to prevent it. It wouldn't work."

Zac paused, considering it. Realization hit him and he closed his eyes in resignation. "It's a paradox, isn't it?" His dad nodded, crossing his arms. "But why can't we at least *try* it? What if all of your theories about creating paradoxes are wrong? What if we don't *injure* time when we change something in the past? Won't time fix itself so that things will go back to normal? Maybe in the new timeline, Chen still goes back to warn us, but it's for a different reason."

His dad stood up and began walking to the living room. "We can't take chances on theories," he said. "If we do something like that, it's not only our lives we're altering through the change. It could possibly be hundreds, even thousands of others. One small change can invariably lead to limitless smaller changes that branch off from the original."

"So let me guess, this all fits into your 'some things are meant to happen a certain way' theory?" His voice was rising. "Because I think it's pretty crappy to think that Rock is 'meant' to be mauled by dinosaurs."

"No, I just want you to get it through your head that some things *are permanent*! There's nothing we can do about them. You found the machine and talked your way into the TEMPUS Project; that's permanent."

"I didn't talk my way into anything!"

"Zac, do you think I'd want my own son getting involved with time travel? The only reason I let you join the team was because I knew Bryce would be able to take care of you. I was afraid that if I didn't let you in on it, you would mess things up worse. It looks like I was right about something!"

Zac was speechless. His eyes fell, and he could feel a lump rising in his throat. His dad must have sensed it, because he immediately began apologizing.

"I didn't mean that. I'm sorry."

"No," Zac said, "I get it. Every word of it. I'm just glad you finally told me what you really think."

"That's not what I really think. I'm just under a tremendous amount of stress right now, and thinking about all of these 'what-ifs' isn't helping. They're not going to fix anything. Right now, I have a bunch of investors I need to answer to who are going to be worrying about a lawsuit, who are going to be worrying about losing their money. I just need some time," he said.

Zac shook his head. "I know I messed things up. So I'm going to fix it."

"Zac, you can't. The damage is already done."

"No," Zac said, turning to go to his room. "I'm going to find a way to fix it, so then you won't be able to blame me anymore."

"You don't even have the Wand anymore. You would need to activate the one I made for you, but I'm not going to allow that."

"Doesn't matter. I'll figure something out. I'll make things right no matter what it takes. Then you'll be able to keep your science project." He smirked as he closed his bedroom door, and then muttered under his breath, "We both know it's what matters to you most."

Zac threw himself onto his bed. He didn't care what his dad said. He was willing to take risks even if his dad wasn't. And if he changed things in the process, how bad could it possibly be? No one could really "injure" *time*. It's not like it was a person or anything. What was the point of having the ability to travel into the past if you couldn't take things that went wrong and make them right again?

Tomorrow, first thing in the morning, he was going to TEMPUS to set things right.

SIXTEEN

Sunday morning, Zac woke up and wasted no time getting to TEMPUS headquarters. He went down the long hallway and found the room darker than normal. The pentagon no longer glowed its aqua color, though the hum of the machine still reverberated throughout the room.

A light was on around the corner where the computers were located. "Hello?" Zac called.

"Yeah," Bryce said. "Come on back. Watch your step."

Zac maneuvered through the hallway to the back room. It was the only room with light, cast from a small overhead lamp and the glow of the screens. Zac took a seat next to Bryce, who was unshaven and looked like he hadn't slept or showered since they arrived back. He smelled like it, too.

"What are you doing?" Zac asked.

"Trying to go through the code," Bryce said. "I told your dad I'd work on it, and I still haven't figured it out." He swore as he scanned the lines of code on the screen.

"I wish I could help you, but I can't understand any of that stuff," Zac said, scanning the code.

"I don't think you'd be able to help anyway," Bryce said. "I can't find anything wrong with it. I need Emilee to help. She was the last one to use the program before we left."

"Have you heard anything else about Rock?" Zac asked.

Bryce shook his head, his eyes fixed on the code displayed on the screen in front of him. "Not much. Emilee texted me to tell me that he's still in the Intensive Care Unit right now. Apparently whatever bit him was poisonous. Of course, the doctors have no idea how to combat that poison since they don't know where it's from, so they're doing all they can to prevent it from spreading to his heart." He sat back and began rubbing his eyes. "Unless I can get Emilee to help me, I think we're just going to have to accept the fact that we may never know what went wrong."

Zac laughed. "Yeah, right. Try telling that to my dad. He's so worried about losing money from all this that he won't stop until everything's perfect."

"I don't know," Bryce said. "I think you ought to give him a bit more credit than that. He's not such a bad guy. Mine was such a deadbeat that he never took care of my mom, never even saw me." He gave a sarcastic laugh. "You know, I'm glad he never came into my life. My mom deserved better. At least the guy at the donut shop was kind to her. *Someone* treated her like she deserved. I always wished I could thank him, that I could let him know what an impact his kindness had. Someday I want to look him up and find him, just to say thanks."

"I'll help you find him," Zac said. "But right now, I need your help to make things right. Right now, the scales are balanced for me."

"What are you talking about?" Bryce asked.

"I've done one good thing with TEMPUS—saving that little girl. And I've messed up once when we tried to go to Roswell and Rock was injured. And now he could die. I can't have it even out like that. I need to do something good once more. I want the good to outweigh the bad if this is going to be shut down."

Bryce shook his head. "I can't let you use it just to help you feel good about yourself," he said. "I don't even have access to the Wands; your dad locked them up and he's the only one who has access to them. So even if I did reactivate TEMPUS, it wouldn't do you any good."

"Bryce, please," Zac pleaded. "I need your help. You have to know some way around all the rules. If I don't fix this, everything just gets worse from here on out for everyone... for my dad, for TEMPUS, for Rock... I don't want it to end like this."

"You know what I think?" Bryce said, turning off the monitor and standing up. He began walking down the hallway and out into the main room, standing in front of the glass cage surrounding the pentagon. "I think you need to just slow down and look at what you've got. Go and make amends with your dad." His words were more urgent, more intense. "Your problem, Zac, is that you're so fixated on your past, on fixing or changing what's already happened. But right now, you're missing a huge opportunity to make things right in your present. Someday you might regret it, might want to go back and make it right, but you have that chance *right now*. You don't need a time machine to do that. So take advantage of it while you can."

"But I don't care about my——"

"You know what my last words were to my mom?" Bryce interrupted. "I told her, 'Don't come back.' We'd been in an argument and she was leaving on a business trip." He looked down, remorse filling his voice. "She never did come back. And every day, I wonder if those last words were how she remembered me. I wish I could go and take those words back, or to tell myself that some of the things I got frustrated about back then weren't worth it. But I can't. What's done is done."

Zac was silent for a while. "I'm sorry," he finally said.

"I know I'm only a couple of years older than you are, but at least hear what I have to say. Don't make the same mistake I did. You still have one parent around, and believe it or not, he *does* care for you. He told me to watch you and to guard your life like I was guarding my own. I'm sure Emilee would gladly trade places with you after all she's been through at the hands of *her* stepfather. I don't know what's worse, having no father in your life, or having one like hers." Bryce began walking through the corridor, up toward the exit.

"Yeah, well," Zac said, calling after him, "we'll see how that goes. No matter what I say or do, it's never going to be good enough. His work is always more important than I am. Sometimes I think I could erase myself from history and he wouldn't even try to stop me."

The school week started out slowly as usual. Zac couldn't stop thinking about all that was happening. Last night, he went straight to his room and got onto his computer, not even bothering to talk to his dad. What did Bryce know, anyway? Bryce only saw one side, the side that loved going to work each day, engrossed with his scientific theories. Not the side that chose science over his own son.

Zac sat alone at lunch, going off to the commons area to eat. He sometimes sat with people from his classes, but the past week he'd been feeling more distant than normal. He'd had less sleep and didn't feel like he fit in with anyone else. He wished he was a few years older like Bryce and Emilee so that he wouldn't have to sit through school anymore. But then there would be college classes to deal with.

At the beginning of one class, Mr. McClane talked with the students about the highlights of their weekends. Zac laughed to himself as his peers described shopping or going to the movies with such enthusiasm that you'd have thought it was the most ground-breaking event imaginable.

"What about you, Zac?" Mr. McClane asked, trying to elicit conversation from him. "What did you do this weekend?"

"Nothing," Zac had said. What was he going to say? He watched his friend get nearly ripped to pieces by dinosaurs in a time travel experiment? Then again, maybe if he told them that, it would get him off the hook. Not like they would believe him anyway. Instead he just stuck with his original answer.

"Suit yourself," Mr. McClane said, shrugging before moving on.

Sitting there in the commons at lunch, Zac noticed students moving toward the televisions, crowding around them. Something was going on. He got up, making his way to one of the flat screen panels mounted above the tables.

"What's going on?" he asked someone. No one answered, and he could see why. They were transfixed, staring intently at the screens. Instead of displaying the daily announcements, the television image was one of a news anchor, text scrolling beneath her as she gave updates on breaking news. Zac listened.

"...No one knows who is responsible for the attack," the anchor said, "but authorities believe this is the work of a cell of domestic terrorists. We do not yet know the number of casualties from the attack, but intelligence sources say that there is credible information to suggest that this is just the beginning of a series of attacks. They have not ruled out the use of biological or chemical weapons. There are also indications that whoever did this may be in possession of sarin gas, a nerve agent…"

Zac stared as the screen displayed image after image of crumbled stone and twisted iron. Investigators in HAZMAT suits combed through the debris, dust swirling in the air. As the camera weaved through the scene, jerky from the movement, Zac thought he could see an arm sticking out from the crushed metal of a subway train. The news anchor continued.

"Reports are coming in from different sources placing the time of the blast at less than an hour ago in Dunham City. Right now, authorities are on the scene trying to determine just *when* the bomb was detonated, but so far, the only thing they are saying is that it happened as the train pulled into the Bishop Street station." The video playing on the screen panned through the carnage, pausing long enough to show a child's stuffed giraffe in the rubble. "They have concluded that the bomb was on one of the subway cars when it went off. We'll keep bringing you more information on this story as it develops."

Zac felt a chill go up his spine. Whoever did this had no regard for innocent children, and if what the news anchor said was true, they could still be out there, possibly with chemical or biological weapons. If they were able to detonate one of those, it would spread through the air, maybe killing hundreds or thousands. He'd seen enough documentaries on television to see what these weapons were capable of. If anything would convince his dad to let him activate TEMPUS and use it, this would be it.

While everyone was gathered in a mob around the television screens, Zac walked through the hallway and snuck out through a side door. He knew he might face repercussions for this act later, but they would be nothing compared to what could happen if these terrorists struck again.

Zac swept through the door to the conference room at TEMPUS headquarters. Everyone except Rock was already there, staring at the television news. No one turned to look at him as he entered. His dad spoke first.

"I know what you're thinking," he said, "but the answer is 'no.'"

Zac walked next to the television hanging on the wall. "What do you mean? Are you seeing what's on the news?"

"Yes," Dr. Ryger said, "and I'm as torn about it as you are, but I'm not willing to risk using a machine that's malfunctioning."

"Then don't risk it yourself," Zac said, gesturing to the television. "Let me do it. Let me see if I can stop the next attack."

"Sit down," his dad said. "Just for a minute."

Chen pushed a chair toward him, and Zac threw himself into it and looked up at the screen. There was no possible way they could ignore this; it had just happened. Situations like this were what the time machine was made for.

"Zac, we've been discussing this since the news started showing the first images," Bryce said. "It's a decision that didn't come easily."

"What, you already made a decision? I thought I was part of the team now, too!"

"You are," his dad said. "But I think we have more experience than you do in this and—"

"So?" Zac said. "Emilee, did you all really agree to this, or did my dad just make you all 'agree to agree' about it?" He looked at her, but she simply looked down at the table.

"I think he's right," she said, barely audible. "After what happened to Rock, I'm afraid that the system might not be ready again."

"But did you check it with Bryce?" he asked. She nodded. "And nothing was wrong?"

"No," Bryce said, speaking for her. "But even though we didn't find anything wrong, we still don't know what made it malfunction like that."

The television news showed even more gruesome footage. Zac couldn't believe they were airing some of the images that they were. But that was what the news did; they used shocking things to get an audience to tune in.

"Just send me in," Zac said. He couldn't stop thinking of the stuffed giraffe, torn from the hands of a child in his or her last seconds of life. "I'm willing to risk it. Look at *that*," he said, standing up again. "And now they say these same terrorists could be in possession of sarin gas! That's nerve gas; we all know what that stuff does."

"It's not that simple," his dad said, trying to dissuade Zac. "We deactivated part of TEMPUS when we did the check through the computer."

"Then reactivate it. How hard can it be?"

"Son, time travel requires a tremendous amount of power, so much that it's basically nuclear. That pentagon that you stand on each time the wormhole is activated is carrying out a continual series of small atomic reactions. It's all safe and contained, but you can't just reactivate the machine and expect it to have enough energy at the start."

Zac ignored him and turned to Bryce. "Come on," he said. "You agree with me. Imagine that your mom was on that train. You said it yourself that you didn't get to say goodbye to her the day she died. I'm sure there are tons of other people today who will be able to relate to you when they identify the bodies." Bryce squirmed in his seat. "And unless we can help get some information on who's behind this, there are going to be a lot more, too." He stood silently, scanning their faces.

Dr. Ryger looked off to the side. Zac couldn't tell what he was thinking, but he knew it was hitting a nerve with the rest of them.

"If you just sit here and do nothing, you're just as guilty as the people who did this," Zac said.

"That's not fair," Emilee said. "It's not that simple of a decision."

"Really?" Zac said, surprised at his directness with her. "Because I think it's such an easy decision and you're all just afraid to make it." He started toward the door. "Well, I'm at least going to decide for myself. I'm going down to the platform and I don't know how, but I'll find a way to reactivate it."

"You can't just go pressing buttons," Chen said. "If you don't calibrate it properly, it'll tear you up when you step into the pentagon."

"Then *help me*. You know how to get it started. Do the right thing, Chen. You said that when you sent us back and Rock was attacked that you did everything right. I believe you, and I want you to do it again." He was at the door now, turning the handle. "Redeem yourself."

"You don't even have another Wand," Emilee said.

"Doesn't matter," Zac said. "A random one worked for me last time. Maybe another one will, too. But no matter what, I'm at least going to *try*." He turned his back and walked out the door, closing it behind him. He was just a few feet away from the entrance behind the bookcase when he heard someone behind him, running to catch up.

"Wait for me." It was Chen. "I'll do it. I'll reactivate it. Your dad is going to throw a fit in a few minutes, but I can at least get you started."

Zac smiled, and they walked down the long hallway together toward the TEMPUS machine.

Chen pulled a chair up to the computer and started typing in a mad rush. Streams of words and numbers scrolled across the screen, and he hit a button hard with finality, then sat back.

A bright blue light lit the room around the corner, and Zac knew it was on again. He patted Chen on the shoulder. "Thanks," he said. He walked over to the case containing the Wands and tried to open it. It was locked. He banged his elbow against the glass, but it didn't budge.

"Wait," a voice said. He turned to see Bryce coming down the walkway with a set of keys. "I'm going with you." He opened the case and took out a Wand.

Zac reached for one, but Bryce held his hand back.

"No," he said. "You need to use your own."

"But I don't have one," Zac said.

Bryce picked one up out of the case and handed it to Zac. "Actually, you do. Your dad was planning on having this one assigned to you so he could figure out why the other one was messing up the way it was. But then after the wormhole malfunctioned the other day, he shut the project down without having this one programmed for you."

"Does he know you're doing this?" Zac asked.

"Yes and no," Bryce replied. "Chen basically told your dad that he was going to make sure you didn't mess things up. I told him I'd check up on you, and then I grabbed the keys. Now come on, let's program your Wand."

Zac followed Bryce to the computers and then watched as Bryce entered some commands into the computer.

"Okay, press your thumb down on it, like you're standing on the pentagon and trying to turn it on," he said. Zac pressed down. Bryce hit a button on the computer, and the lights on the side of the device illuminated. "You can remove your thumb now," he said.

Zac held the device up and looked at it. The last Wand worked by accident; this one was *designed* to work for him. He smiled, then walked into the chamber to prepare.

"Give it about three more minutes," Chen said. "Then it should be stable enough to use."

Zac turned to face Bryce, who stood outside the glass doors. "Okay, so what's the plan?"

"Plan?" Bryce asked. "I'm following *you* this time."

Zac crossed his arms and breathed heavily, thinking. "We need to get to the subway station and look for anything suspicious. The news said it wasn't a suicide bomber, so whoever did it planted it and left. We can have Chen drop us somewhere on the subway platform. I think we should look for someone at the station right before it detonated."

"How do you know they got on at that station and not an earlier one?"

"I don't," Zac said. "But here's what I'm thinking... security is tight on public transit, right?" Bryce nodded. "So if whoever put the bomb on there really wants it to go off, they're not going to give the authorities time to find it first. If they put it on the subway car right before they want it to blow up, there's a good chance no one will notice it in time."

"They have video surveillance they can just look at, though," Chen said from around the corner. "Why not just let them identify the bomber that way."

"We can make a positive identification much more quickly," Zac said. "We don't have to rely on video footage to get the details; we can see them up close. We can watch for signs of someone acting

137

suspicious. If we can figure out who did it, we can tell the authorities who to look at on the footage, help them narrow down their search time. I think it's worth a try."

"Okay," Bryce said. "But I just want to make sure we're doing the right thing. If something goes wrong and we're on the subway train when the bomb goes off, it's over for us. And I don't mean the machine will just bring us back here."

"I know," Zac said.

"And another thing: if we call in information about the bomber, how are we going explain what we know? This is different than the types of observations we've done before."

Zac shrugged. "Maybe it's time to let more people know about TEMPUS. Maybe my dad might have to give up his secret."

Chen called from around the corner. "It's stable," he said. "I've got it set to place you in a crowd, so be careful. That location's so crowded in the morning that no one should notice you suddenly appearing, but you need to recover right away."

"Got it," Zac said. He walked into the chamber. Bryce followed him. "Here we go, I guess." He held up the Wand and prepared to activate it.

Bryce grabbed his hand. "Wait," he said. "You realize that if your dad finds out we lied, he's going to shut this down for good, and he won't let us have access anymore. So hopefully he doesn't come down here and find us gone before the machine brings us back five minutes from now."

"Yeah, I know," Zac said. He paused. "And sorry for that comment I made about your mom in the conference room."

Bryce looked away momentarily. "That *was* pretty low," he said, "but you made a good point. So let's do this and get back here before your dad finds out."

They pressed their thumbs to the Wands and vanished.

138

SEVENTEEN

Zac's stomach churned as his feet hit something hard. He opened his eyes and saw that he was in the back of a crowd. In front of him, people stood waiting for the subway in what felt like an underground cavern. Ancient yellowing lights cast a glow all around him. This part of the subway was in an older tunnel. That was probably why the terrorists chose it, he thought. Its structure would be weaker, causing more damage.

He felt a tap on his shoulder. Bryce whispered into his ear. "What are we looking for?" All around them were travelers with laptop cases, backpacks, briefcases, and purses. How could they identify a lone person with a suspicious bag?

"Start walking around and looking," he said. "Hopefully whoever did it is still here somewhere. Look for someone who is acting strange. If you think you found the suspect, meet back over here." He glanced up at the digital clock on the wall. "Looks like we have about eight minutes before the subway train arrives."

They split up and began searching. Zac made his way through the crowd, trying to look as casual as possible. His eyes searched individuals up and down. No one looked out of the ordinary. A few people checked their watches, but that was nothing unusual. People were impatient.

Zac looked up at the clock. Four minutes left until the subway train arrived. Time was running out. He turned to check behind him, to see if anyone was coming down the stairs, but they were empty. He saw no sign of Bryce, either.

Out of the corner of his eye, he noticed something. A man was carrying a normal, black leather briefcase, but something was different about him. Zac moved closer.

He was wearing blue jeans and a dark blue windbreaker. A black baseball hat covered his head, short brown hair sticking out of it. He wore ear buds like most travelers, listening to music, but it was the side of his head that caught Zac's attention the most. Running down the man's temples and across the bridge of his nose were droplets of sweat. The subway tunnel was cold, but the man was sweating like it was the middle of the summer. He rose up and down on the balls of his feet like he was nervous. The man gripped the handle of the briefcase with two hands, one over the other, and held it in front of him. His fingers shook slightly.

The strangest thing, Zac thought, was that he seemed to be staring straight ahead, as if he didn't want to draw any attention to himself. Like he was the only one down there.

The man's eyes moved to the side and caught a glimpse of Zac, then quickly focused straight in front again.

Zac looked away, then began stepping forward, casting a glance sideways. The man's eyes met Zac's, and he turned his head with a jerk, looking away.

A loud vibrating noise filled the tunnel, and the train pulled into the station, slowing down with a hiss of air brakes in front of the platform. A voice came over the intercom announcing the next stop, and people began surging forward.

"Zac, over here!" He turned to see Bryce motioning for him, and walked over. "See anything?"

"Yeah," Zac said. "There's something suspicious going on with that guy." He turned and pointed, but the man was gone. "Wait; he was there a minute ago. Where'd he go?"

"Did you get a good look?"

"Sort of," Zac replied, "but I want to see if he leaves that briefcase of his. Go ahead and return to TEMPUS, and I'll leave in just a few seconds. I want to get another glance."

"You sure?"

"Yeah. It'll only take me a minute. And technically, I'll be arriving back at the same time you do anyway." Bryce nodded and went into a secluded corner. When he thought no one was looking in his direction, he pressed the top of the Wand and was gone.

Zac moved along with the crowd, searching for the man in the windbreaker. Where had he gone? He scanned the crowd for anyone wearing blue, but he couldn't find anything. He neared the subway train as the rest of the people were boarding, and looked into the windows. He pulled out the Wand and prepared to activate it.

He felt a hand grab his hair and slam his face against the outside of the train. His head was pressed against it sideways, and all he could see was the tunnel snaking off into the distance. A voice whispered in his ear.

"You think you're clever, don't you? You think I don't know a badge when I see one?" He dug his hands into Zac's hair, pulling it at the roots. He used his other hand to pin Zac's arm behind his back. Zac gripped the Wand.

"I'm not a cop," Zac said through gritted teeth, trying not to focus on the pain. "I'm just a teenager. I don't know what you're talking about."

"Don't play dumb with me," the man said. "I saw you eyeballing me back there. You think you seen something? What's this?" he asked, and pried the Wand from Zac's hand.

Zac's eyes widened with fear. He had to get it back before it was too late. "I know what you're planning," he said, taking a chance. He could hear the crowd thinning out as everyone got on board.

"Oh, really?" The man let go of his hair and spun Zac around to face him. They were eye to eye now. Zac could feel the man's breath on his face as he spoke. "You think you're gonna stop us? This is just the beginning. What is this thing, anyway?" He held up the Wand. "Some kind of tiny camera? You taking pictures or something? I'll show you what you can do with your little pictures." He threw the Wand through the open door of the subway train and watched it roll across the floor, between the feet of the passengers and out of sight. The man shoved Zac forward through the door.

Zac spun around, hearing a hiss as the doors closed, and he could see the man on the outside, watching him. The man waved, and Zac could feel his weight shift as the subway train began to move.

He searched the floor for the Wand, but he didn't see it. Passengers gave him dirty looks as he scrambled around their feet, excusing himself and looking under seats. One woman screamed, and he gave a fake smile. "Sorry," he said. "I dropped my, uh... pen..." He crawled along the floor to get a better look, trying not to think about how filthy it was. It smelled like someone had recently vomited on it. But that wouldn't matter in the next few minutes if he couldn't find the Wand. Somehow it had gotten kicked around in there, and time was running out.

142

He began to wonder if he'd get out of this alive. Under one seat, he saw something slender and black and reached for it, stretching until his fingers were barely touching it.

The train lurched to the side and the Wand moved, rolling out of reach. Zac cursed under his breath and got up on his knees, looking around. He said nothing, but he looked to the other passengers as if pleading for their help. Then he saw it.

The Wand had stopped at the feet of a passenger with small shoes that sparkled and lit up every time she moved them. Zac's glance moved up, and he saw that it was a little girl. In her hands, she held a stuffed giraffe.

The child bent down to pick up the pen-like object. She stood up to take it to Zac, but her mother started to pull her back down. The little girl slipped from her mom's grip and handed Zac the device.

"Thank you," he said, grabbing it with his right hand. A sick feeling formed in his gut as he realized what was about to happen.

A voice came over the intercom, announcing that they were approaching the next stop. The bomb would detonate any minute now, maybe in a matter of seconds. Zac took one last look around at the people around him, oblivious that these precious few seconds were about to be their last. No final goodbyes to their loved ones. No time to prepare to face their Maker. Just death.

Unexpected, violent, unnecessary death. He placed his thumb on the top of the Wand and took a deep breath.

"I'm sorry," Zac said, a tear forming in his eye as he watched the little girl cuddle the stuffed giraffe. He hesitated a moment.

Finally, he squeezed his eyes tight, a tear running down his cheek. He pressed the sensor on the top of the Wand, and as he did so, he felt a burst of heat and could sense a bright light through his closed eyelids.

• • •

Zac arrived back on the platform and collapsed. Bryce stood next to him and grabbed him by the arm, pulling him up.

"You okay?" he asked. "What happened?"

Zac pushed past him and walked out into the open room. He paced back and forth, eyes clouding with tears, and he reached up to wipe them away.

"Zac, what happened back there? Is something wrong?"

"Yes!" Zac shouted and spun around, fist slamming into the thick glass pane. It shook but did not break. His words echoed off the walls. "Everything's wrong!" He shook his head. "Children, Bryce... innocent *children* were killed today, and I couldn't do a *thing* about it." He gritted his teeth and continued pacing, his feet landing hard on the concrete. "I had to look this little girl in the eyes... she... she walked right up to me... and..." Zac struggled to find the words to say, "...and she was holding her stuffed animal, so small and sweet and then..." He took a deep breath and continued talking and pacing, not looking up to meet Bryce's stare. "Why couldn't I even save *one* child? Would it really matter? Why couldn't I just... why couldn't I do what you and Emilee did to save me and Rock, just take her with me? Would it really make a difference?"

Bryce listened in silence.

"I just don't get it," Zac said. He rubbed his eyes. "I mean, you should have seen the way she looked at me. She had no idea that her life was going to end in a matter of seconds." He laughed to himself. "It's my own fault, really. I went into this situation knowing what would happen to those people. But to see them all looking at me, their eyes... And I was helpless to do anything." His shoulders sank.

He looked up, not realizing that Chen had left the computers and had stepped into the room.

"Sorry," Chen said. "Did you get what you needed?"

144

He nodded, still feeling sick to his stomach. "I think so. This guy, he confronted me and thought I was an undercover police officer." Zac left out the part about almost losing his Wand and not making it back.

"Just give me the description," Chen said, "and I'll go call it in. You just need to calm down right now."

Zac told him what he could remember, what the man looked and sounded like, and Chen left the room.

"I know how you feel," Bryce finally said, speaking softly. "It's miserable. And I've seen far more than you have."

"But nothing this bad," Zac said. "You guys have been able to *stop* crimes from going any further. I had to watch this little girl and all these other people face their last minutes before being blown to bits. I stood with them, and I was able to escape, but not them. It's not fair."

"I know," Bryce said, "but I don't think you really realize all that the rest of us have seen while we've worked on this project. You've been here for only a week. Try doing this for a year or two."

"I don't know if I can," Zac said. "Not if it's going to be stuff like this. I'm starting to wonder if it would be better if this whole TEMPUS thing was never built in the first place. I'm starting to think maybe it's all a big mistake."

"Zac," Bryce interrupted, frustration filling his voice, "you're not the only person to have these doubts. You're acting like you're the only one who has seen anything horrible or who has had any doubts about it all. You think it's easy for *any* of us to see these things? You think you're the only one who would love to go and change the past?"

"I think—"

"You've witnessed something horrible, but at least it's not someone you know." Zac had never seen Bryce this agitated. "I'd *love* to go back and see my mom one more time. I'd *love* to change the last thing I said to her. But instead, I get to watch her die over and over and over again while *you* sit and talk about how you want to find ways to change things in the past. But it's *not going to happen!* You have to face the fact that you're using a *time machine.* You crossed that threshold when you stepped onto the platform and used that Wand." He thrust his finger at Zac. "You volunteered to join the team, and you need to realize that there are some things that just are a part of the job. You're going to have to see things you're not going to want to see, and you need to *deal* with it. There are times I wish I'd never set foot in this building, either. But it's too late."

Zac avoided eye contact with Bryce, choosing instead to gaze down at the floor. Something had set him off.

"I know you want to go back and save your mom," Bryce said, "but at least you had a good life with her. You don't live every day with the regret of your last words to your mom, replaying them in your mind every time you watch her die."

"What do you mean?" Zac said. His voice was soft, careful.

Bryce leaned against the wall, then collapsed, sinking to the floor. "I'd rather not talk about it."

"I have dreams about my mom dying, too," Zac offered. "Almost every night, I replay it in my head, every bit of it. It's always muddled, and I don't remember the details. I just remember her getting shot in a crowded place and falling to the ground, and then my dad attacking the guy. And then it usually ends."

"I'm not talking about dreams," Bryce said. "I get to revisit my mom's last moments every time I watch those planes crash into the towers. I get to hear myself say, 'Don't come back,' and wonder if that's the last thing she thought about me. If she really believed I meant it." He sniffed and wiped his shirt sleeve across his eyes. "Well, she didn't come back. And every time I see it, it doesn't get easier. It just gets worse. Every time is a reminder to me of what I did, a little stab in the heart to rub it in. And I can never take it back."

Zac sat down next to him. "I'm sorry," he said. "I didn't realize. Haven't you told my dad? You can't keep doing this to yourself."

"I need to," Bryce said. "I hate it, and it makes me hate myself, but it shows me who I really am deep down inside. Hateful, angry... and no matter how many times I watch it, I know it wasn't the terrorists flying those planes into the buildings that killed her that day. I did."

Zac shook his head. "You can't blame yourself," he said. "We've all done things we regret."

"I seriously doubt that it was as bad as what I did. I can't be forgiven for what I said to her."

"So is that why you joined TEMPUS?" Zac asked. "To make amends?"

Bryce didn't answer, but stood up and started up the ramp to the main office.

EIGHTEEN

Zac sat in the conference room and watched the news, hoping to see some sign that the people responsible for the subway attack would be caught. He knew that the police wouldn't tell the media what kinds of leads they had received. It would only cause those who did it to go into hiding. But he had hope.

He walked over to the couch alongside the wall and lay down, putting his hands behind his head and keeping his eyes trained on the scrolling updates on the television. It would take time, of course. But he didn't want to see anyone else get hurt.

His eyes became heavy, and he began to close them, slipping into sleep.

He was back on the subway train. He sat in one of the seats, riding along. The movement of the train tossed him gently from side to side as it moved along the tracks. He felt a tug at his sleeve.

He looked down and saw the little girl from the train. "Hi," she said. "What's your name?"

"Um… Zac," he said.

She smiled. "Mine's Samantha. Today, I get to go see my daddy at work. We're gonna have lunch together!" She leaned against her mom's side.

"Honey," her mother said, "leave the man alone. He doesn't want to be bothered."

"It's okay," Zac said. "I don't mind."

The woman smiled. "She's been talking about this for days. Her father's always working, and he's been out of town for a week. They've been video-chatting for days, and now she's ecstatic because she gets to spend some time with him."

"I understand," Zac said. "Where are you going to get lunch?"

"A pizza place!" the little girl exclaimed. "My favorite."

"Yeah," Zac replied, "I like pizza too."

The girl's demeanor became serious. Her gaze fell to her lap, and her stuffed giraffe hung at her knees. "Why are you leaving us?" she asked.

"What?"

"I won't get to see my daddy. He's going to miss us. And you're leaving."

"What are you talking about?" Zac asked.

The girl began screaming hysterically. The mom didn't seem to notice. Zac tried to calm the girl down, to reassure her, but suddenly the mother began screaming, too.

One by one, the passengers in the subway train opened their mouths and let out blood-curdling shrieks. Zac jerked his head back and forth, looking between them. His heart began beating harder, and he stood up, turning around.

A bald man stood up and came near him, standing face to face. His mouth was open in a loud yell, and in an instant, blood ran down his face.

The floor of the train ignited, flames licking the passengers. Zac clamped his hands over his ears, shutting his eyes. He could feel the hands of the passengers grabbing his shirt and pants, tugging at him, pulling him down with them. He struggled against it, and began screaming himself.

He woke to find a hand on his arm. Bryce stood over him, shaking him. "You okay?" he asked.

Zac sat up and examined his surroundings. His heart pounded, and he was covered in sweat. "Huh? Yeah," he said. "It was a nightmare. About the subway."

Bryce sat down next to him. "I've had those."

Zac was still breathing hard; his hands were shaking.

"Look, I'm sorry for going off on you earlier," he said. "I don't talk about my mom much. The only other person who knows how she died is Rock."

"It's okay," Zac said, rubbing the sleep from his eyes. "I guess I deserved it."

"No, you didn't. But we've got bigger things to deal with right now. It's Emilee."

"What?" Zac sat up. "What happened to her?"

"Nothing yet," Bryce said. "It's what she did."

"What do you mean?"

Bryce sighed. "She saw me storming out of the building after I talked to you. She tried to calm me down, and we went out to eat. She told me that Rock's recovering, but he's going to need some physical therapy. The poison was a neurotoxin, so it messed up his nerves. He may never get full use of his arm back."

Zac hung his head.

"We started talking, and I told her about what you and I were talking about, how it's tough to accept that we can't change the past and what happened. And then she just broke down and started crying."

"About what?" Zac asked.

"She didn't really say, but I think it was about her stepfather. With Rock being hurt, I think it touched a nerve or something. She said something about hating how things turned out, something about her brother. And then said she was going to make sure it didn't happen."

"But you think she was talking about her stepfather?"

Bryce nodded. "I think that's what she meant. I think she wants to change things so he never hurts her or her brother."

Zac's thoughts wandered to Emilee and how distant she was when he brought up her brother. He glanced up at the television screen. Still no breaking news saying that those responsible for the subway attack had been caught. He had to give it time. He wished he could jump ahead to the future to see what happens.

"So what did Emilee do that's so important?" Zac asked.

"She used the machine," Bryce said. "I think she's going back to stop her stepfather."

"When?"

"Just now."

Zac jumped up. "She can't do that. If she changes something, it can cause a wound in time."

"She may already have," Bryce said. "It may be bleeding through right now and we just don't realize it."

"I have to stop her," Zac said.

"You can't," Bryce said. "Whatever she did, wherever she went... there's nothing we can do."

"Sure there is," Zac said, walking toward the door. "I can just have the machine send me to the last-known coordinates. If she's there, I can stop her before she changes anything. Maybe she hasn't succeeded yet; everything seems the same right now."

"Or maybe…" Bryce said, then hesitated.

"Maybe what?"

"Maybe something happened to her. Maybe that's why we don't see any changes."

A chill ran up his spine. If what Bryce said about Emilee's stepfather was true and he did something to her… Zac shook the thought off.

"I have to do something," Zac said. "I need someone to send me to those coordinates. Where's Chen? Where's my dad?"

"Chen went home. Your dad was pretty angry at him for sending you to the subway like that."

"What about my dad?"

"He's not happy with you, either. He saw that you were sleeping so he went to go smooth things over with Rock's parents. But when he gets back, I think you're going to get an earful."

Zac shook his head. "It doesn't matter. I need you to set the machine for me," he said. "There has to be a way for you to tell it to send me to the same time Emilee arrived." He stepped into the hallway.

Bryce thought. "I don't know," he said. "It's possible, but I don't know if it can be the same exact moment."

"Come on," Zac said. "You worked on the machine's programming. Don't tell me you can't figure *something* out." He was at the bookcase now and tugged at it, sliding it open. He headed down the concrete ramp.

"Okay, I'll try," Bryce said. "Emilee would know how. But I can try to get you as close to the place as possible. But once you're in the past with her, how will you find her?"

"I don't know," Zac said, opening the case and grabbing the Wand. "I'll figure something out. But I have this horrible gut feeling that she got in way over her head, and now she's in trouble." He hurried around the corner and pointed to the computer screen. "Get it set," he said. "Please. After this, I won't ask for anything else." He looked Bryce directly in the eye. "But I need to stop her."

Bryce moved to the computer and sat down, pulling the keyboard toward him. "Okay," he said. "I'll do what I can. But there's no guarantee. When this thing malfunctioned the other day, I wondered if Emilee was somehow responsible for it. She might have altered the programming so that no one can stop her."

Zac nodded and headed around the corner toward the pentagon. "Yell when it's ready." He stood outside the glass door, waiting for it to open. He fidgeted with the Wand, moving it back and forth between his fingers.

The hum grew louder and the door swung open. "You're online!" Bryce yelled. "Good luck. It'll set you somewhere in the vicinity of where she landed."

Zac stood in the center of the platform. He looked down at the blue light, the dark swirls moving beneath his feet. "Here goes nothing," he said to himself. He pushed his thumb down on the device.

Something felt different this time. His body was still tossed and jerked around, but it felt strange. Unfamiliar.

The world slowly came into focus, and he steadied himself and began looking around. He was in a metallic room. Bright white lights shone overhead, and he could see several metal tables supported by a base filled with drawers. Next to each table were wide silver trays.

To his left, he saw a door with fogged windows, the kind of glass that lets light in but obscures what is inside. Something to his right caught his eye. Filling the wall were doors of what looked to be

153

giant filing cabinets. Zac approached them. They were bigger than anything he had seen before, but they looked familiar. Like he had seen them somewhere before in a movie or a television show.

He stood in front of one and grabbed the handle. He checked behind him; no one was there. With great care not to be heard, he pulled on the drawer.

The pale face of a woman with her eyes closed faced him. He recoiled in horror and shut the door with a loud *slam*. He immediately started shaking. It was a dead body. He was in a morgue. That's what those drawers were for—bodies.

Could Emilee be in one of them? He shuddered to think that he might need to open every one of them to check for her. Was he too late?

A whining noise startled him, and he saw the door across the room slide open and into the wall. A man with a graying beard and in a doctor's coat entered.

"Can I help you?" he asked. "What are you doing in here? Do I need to call security?"

"No!" Zac said. "I can explain. I... got lost while looking for a friend. I wandered in here by accident."

The man gave him a puzzled look. "You shouldn't even be on this floor," he said. "The visitor's kiosk is on the sixteenth floor."

"Visitor's kiosk?"

"Are you looking for a patient?" the man asked. He held up his clipboard, which was clear and thin. Zac could see his shoes on the floor beneath it. The man touched the surface of it, and it came to life, lighting up in the center with a computer screen. "I can check for you," the man said. "Tell me his name."

"Uh..." Zac hesitated. This sounded like a hospital, but why would Emilee go to a hospital? "That's okay," he said, watching the words scroll down the clipboard like a computer screen. "I think I'll just go back up to the sixteenth floor and check the kiosk. Thanks for your time." He turned to walk out the door and headed to the right.

The man chased after him. "Sir," he said, "the elevator's in the other direction."

Zac shook his head as if he were simply confused and headed the other way. "Long day," he said. "Sorry." The man eyed him suspiciously. As Zac headed toward the elevator at the end of the hallway, he looked back to see the man watching him. He came to the elevator and pressed the button.

The door shot open faster than any elevator he'd ever seen. The walls inside of it were made of a smooth, black surface. The buttons on the side weren't buttons at all, but rather a touchscreen panel with lit numbers beneath the transparent surface of the wall. He gave it a curious look and pushed the number sixteen.

Right before the door closed, he could see the man down the hall staring at him, talking down into the clipboard. A feeling of dread filled his stomach.

The elevator shot up, and Zac fell to the floor. It came to a sudden stop within five seconds, throwing him off balance. The door opened again. A woman was waiting outside and stared at him as if he were from another planet.

"Are you okay?" she asked.

"Uh, yeah," Zac said. "I just slipped." He pushed himself to his feet and stepped out. "Thanks." The woman stepped into the elevator and the doors closed.

Zac turned around and took in his surroundings. He walked around the corner toward the hallway, and pure white walls stretched on for what looked like a mile. He knew his eyes must be playing tricks on him.

He started walking, and the wall changed to reveal a person that began talking to him. "Greetings," the woman in the wall said. Zac looked behind him, not sure if it was talking to him or someone else. "Welcome to Carter Memorial Hospital. Please select an option from the menu." The wall next to the woman became a screen, and Zac stared at it. It looked like a web page with its layout.

Suddenly it struck him that this couldn't have been where Emilee had gone. This kind of technology wasn't around when she was a kid. So why was he here? Had she put it in here as a "trap" of sorts so that anyone who tried to stop her couldn't? Where was he?

When was he?

Zac looked at the options on the menu. He had to start somewhere. If Emilee was in here, maybe her name was listed.

"Please select an option from the menu," the voice repeated.

"Patient directory," Zac said out loud and waited. Nothing happened. He repeated it, louder and more clearly.

"Please select an option from the menu."

A man walked up next to Zac and pressed the wall where it said "Patient Directory." The wall reconfigured into a different screen.

"Having trouble?" the man asked.

"Yeah, thanks," Zac said. "I've never used one of these before."

The man laughed. "That's funny. Your folks must be pretty wealthy to have already upgraded to a voice-activated wall system at home."

"Voice activated?"

"Not many of us have the new voice systems. Most houses just have these standard interactive walls. But I guess you rich kids don't realize how it is for the rest of us."

Zac stared at the wall. "Um… does this thing have a calendar on it so I can… check something?"

The man reached over and pressed some spaces on the wall. The menu disappeared and a calendar popped up. It was the same day as when he left. But the year was what shocked him.

Somehow, the TEMPUS machine had propelled him about one hundred and fifty years into the future.

NINETEEN

Zac took a step back. How had this happened? Why would Emilee visit the future? What was she trying to accomplish?

Or what if the computer malfunctioned again? Instead of sending him to the past, it sent him ahead? He excused himself from the man and snuck around the corner, pulling out the Wand. He had to get back to talk to Bryce; something had gone wrong. He pressed down on the sensor.

Nothing happened. He tried again. Still nothing.

He examined the device and saw that the lights were not working. Did it mean that it was out of power? He moved down the hallway, the images on the wall flickering and changing into different things: pictures of animals, advertisements and posters, interactive screens… he leaned against the wall to think.

"Invalid selection," the voice around him said. "Please make another choice. Invalid selection."

A doctor came out of a room, holding another see-through digital clipboard. "Don't lean against the wall, please," he said and shook his head.

Shaken, Zac stood back up. He looked down the hallway and could see what looked like a multitude of rooms, each one packed together and tiny. He started walking, hoping to find an exit. He looked down at the Wand; one bar was lit up now.

Zac breathed a sigh of relief. It was still working. At least partially. He tried pushing the sensor, but still, nothing happened.

A nurse passed him. "Doctor," she said, peeking into one of the rooms, "the Jane Doe in 1623 is still suffering some side effects from the trauma. She keeps saying that she needs to get back to her own time."

"Just give her a mild sedative until we can run some scans," the doctor replied. "She's been talking like that since she was admitted. The person who dropped her off said he found her passed out."

The nurse nodded and tapped something onto her clipboard. "It's being administered right now," she said. "I'm scheduling another scan." She lowered the board to her side and walked on.

Zac stopped. Could it be? Was Emilee here? But why was she a patient?

He waited until the doctor was out of sight and moved down the hallway, toward room 1623. Other people walked in and out of the rooms as he passed, family and friends coming to wish a speedy recovery or to visit. Room 1623 was toward the end of the hallway. He passed door after door, occasionally pausing to glance inside.

"Watch out," someone said, and Zac pressed himself to the side, careful to avoid touching the wall again. A few men pushed a bed past him with an elderly man on it. Zac had to stop and look again. It looked like the bed was levitating, just floating in mid-air.

But that was impossible. Yet there it was, being guided along by a gentle push of the hand.

Finally, he came to the door of the room. Zac looked behind him, making sure no one saw him going in. Then again, in this place, they probably had cameras everywhere, even inside the walls.

The room was dark except for a red light in the corner. A lone bed lay in the center of the room, an IV drip hanging down next to it. There were no heart monitors or machines beeping and cluttering up the room. Instead, the wall next to the bed glowed with numbers and moving lines, about ten screens spread across the surface.

Zac moved closer, stepping in to get a better look at Jane Doe. Her bed did not levitate like the one he saw in the hallway. Instead, it rested on top of a rectangular base that was the same size. Before he could get any closer, he heard a soft, croaking voice coming from the bed.

"Zac?"

Zac ran up to her. "Emilee? What are you doing here?"

She gave a weak smile, then reached up to touch his face. "Hey, there…"

"Emilee, why did you use TEMPUS? What were you *thinking*? You're lucky I was able to find you!"

Emilee just turned over like she was half asleep. Zac shook her.

"You need to get up. We have to get back. The machine malfunctioned again, and my device is having trouble working. Where's yours?"

Emilee said nothing, but began drifting off, her eyes glazing over. "So sweet…" she said. "…that's why I like you so much…"

Zac looked at the wall that displayed the screens. Her heart rate was slowing as she fell into a sleeping pattern. He had to wake her up or he might never get her out of there and back home. He looked at her IV drip. It was giving her a steady dose of something. He followed the tube down to her arm and pulled off the tape, slowly easing the needle out of her vein. He grabbed a cotton ball and pressed it to her skin.

"Come on," he said. "I need you to wake up. You're not supposed to be here." He lifted her and she stumbled out of the bed. She was still groggy and sleepy. "We need you to get dressed. Here, put these on." He handed her the jeans that were in the closet.

Emilee slid the small plastic monitor off her finger and struggled to put the clothes on. She began to become more awake, more aware of her surroundings. "Where am I?" she asked.

Zac slipped her shoes on her feet, and she looked around the room, confused. "You're the one who got here first. You tell me."

Emilee squeezed her eyes shut and grabbed her head in pain. She grunted. "Someone did this."

"Who?" Zac prodded. "Bryce thought you used the machine to go back and stop your stepfather."

"What?" Emilee said, puzzled, "No. No, I didn't use the machine."

"Then how'd you get here? The doctors said someone brought you here; did something happen after you left?"

"No," Emilee said, shaking her head. "I told you, I didn't use the machine. I just... After you stormed off to go try and stop the subway bombing, I talked with your dad for a while, and then I left." She paused, her memories becoming clearer. "I just remember someone putting something over my mouth, and then I passed out. When they brought me in, I tried to tell them I'm not supposed to be here." Her eyes widened, and she tried standing up. "Someone brought me here."

"Who did?"

"I don't know," she said. "I tried talking to the doctor and then..." she stopped suddenly, then rushed over to the table, a look of horror spreading to her face. "Oh, no." She held up a small cylindrical object. Her Wand.

It was crushed in the middle.

"That isn't..."

Emilee nodded. "The doctor told me that when I was brought in, it was all I had with me. What do I do?"

The monitors on the wall started beeping, calling the nurses to check on the patient. Zac looked outside the door. A nurse was walking down the hallway.

"Here," Zac said, tossing her the shirt from the closet. "Put this on; we've gotta get out of here."

"Just use your Wand," Emilee said, pulling her shirt on.

"I can't," Zac said. "For some reason, it's not working in here. I think something's interfering with it. We have to get out of here." He stepped out the door. Emilee followed.

"Excuse me," said the nurse. She called after them. "Wait a minute! You can't just leave!"

Zac looked back, then started running. He paused. Emilee was still feeling the effects of whatever they dosed her with. He hurried back and slung her arm over his shoulder. "Come on," he said. "I've got you."

They hurried down the hallway toward the end of the corridor; there was a stairwell there. The walls immediately lit up all around him, covered in security camera footage of Zac leading Emilee out of her room just moments ago.

Zac stood in front of the stairwell door, looking for a handle to push open. He put his hand to it, pushing.

Instantly, the door slid sideways into the wall, and they stepped through. The stairwell was steep; they were on the sixteenth floor.

"What do we do?" Emilee asked. She looked down at the spiraling staircase.

"Do you think you can walk?"

"I..." she braced herself, grabbing onto the railing. "I think so."

"Good. Let's go." Together they scrambled down the stairs. Zac looked down and saw some men coming up the stairs. "Great," he said. "New plan."

At the next floor, he touched the door, and it slid open.

"What are you doing?" Emilee asked.

"They're looking for us on the stairs. We need to get back on the elevator. You're going to have to run for it. Can you do that?"

She nodded. "Ready?" she asked.

"Ready," Zac said. "On the count of three. One... two..."

Emilee bolted down the hallway, pushing aside a levitating bed and almost knocking someone over.

Zac hurried and followed; people stared at them, many yelling obscenities. Few seemed to notice the walls that displayed images of them leaving her room just minutes earlier. Everyone was probably so used to the walls displaying pictures that they just ignored them. At least Zac and Emilee could hope that was the case.

They reached the elevator and got in, the sleek black doors shutting behind them. Zac checked the Wand; the lights were all out again.

"This isn't good," he said. "Something's not right." He pressed the illuminated button on the wall, and the doors closed.

They felt a fast sinking sensation as the elevator dropped to the first floor. The elevator stopped, but the door remained closed. A voice came out of nowhere, seemingly emanating from the walls.

"Hospital staff and patrons please observe," it said. The black wall was filled with a glowing white square about thirty inches across. "There has been a security breach. Please take note of the individual in question and report any sighting immediately." The image changed to a picture of Emilee's face. It looked like it was

163

from a security camera, zoomed in and cleaned up to give a crystal-clear shot of her. Under her picture were the words "Considered Dangerous."

"What does that mean?" Emilee asked. "Why are they calling it a security breach?"

"I don't know," Zac said. "How did you get here? Did you get yourself in trouble or something?"

She shook her head, staring at her image in the wall. "No, I keep telling you. I didn't use TEMPUS. I don't know how I ended up here."

The door to the elevator opened and the screen disappeared from the wall, becoming a shade of obsidian again. Zac noticed some people walking their way.

"Okay," he said. "We need to do this quickly. See the doors at the opposite end of the room?"

Emilee gazed through the massive, open lobby. To the right was a cafeteria; to the left was a gift shop. Farther past that, she could see what looked like a check-in station for incoming patients. The doors were just beyond the desk, a security guard stationed nearby. The guard was watching the monitors carefully, bending down to examine them. "I see the doors," she said. "Do we make a run for it?"

Zac shook his head. "No, that'll draw attention. We need to act calmly. Keep your head down." He started down the hallway, walking as slowly as he could, but occasionally looking up to see if anyone was following or otherwise watching.

Emilee followed. They passed the cafeteria and the gift shop. The loud noise poured from the cafeteria and no one seemed to notice them. And why would they? They were eating.

Zac moved toward the check-in station. Hospital employees were talking with other patients, handing them digital clipboards to fill out information. One woman looked up from typing on hers and smiled. Zac smiled back.

"There's no way we're going to get past that guy," Emilee said, eyes darting toward the security guard. Zac turned and faced her. "We can't just walk right out. He's going to recognize me right away."

"Well," Zac said, "do you have a better idea?"

Emilee thought for a moment. "Come here," she said. "Put your arm around my waist." She lifted her arm up so he could move in close. "Now pull me in, like we're a couple."

Zac's heart skipped a beat as he held her close. He felt the same as he did when they escaped on the cliff together just a few days ago. "What are we doing?"

"Pretend you're in love with me," she said. She put her arms around his neck and intertwined her hands together. Lowering her head, she rested it on his chest, hiding her face.

Zac could smell her hair. He pulled her in by the waist a little closer and started walking, lowering his head down to touch her forehead.

"Good," she whispered. "Just play along." Both of their faces were slightly hidden as they approached the security guard.

Zac's hands trembled slightly as they neared the door. They were so close.

Suddenly, Emilee pulled away, giggling, her hands held out in a defensive position. She looked down at her feet, and her long black hair hung down in front of her face. "Stop tickling me!" she said, voice filled with laughter.

Zac caught on; he reached out as if he was going to tickle her again. She dodged and moved out of the way, then ran for the door.

"No!" she said playfully. "Stop it!"

"Fine," Zac said, running after her like he was going to tickle her again. Emilee let out a squeal and passed through the doors as they opened for her.

The security guard looked up from the computer monitors, chuckled, and mumbled something about "lovebirds."

Once outside, Zac stopped and stared while Emilee laughed. Her smile was enormous, bigger than he'd ever seen before.

"How... how'd you do that?" he asked.

"What?" she asked, becoming serious again. She started walking.

"That little scene back there? I've never seen you act like that."

Emilee shrugged. "I took drama back in high school. Junior year. By the way, nice job pretending to be in love with me."

"Uh, yeah..."

She stopped, staring straight ahead. "Wow..."

Zac stared, too. The city in front of them was alive with activity. While it was nothing like in the cartoons that took place in the future, it was still bright and vibrant. It was nothing like the dark, dystopian futures he had read about in novels at school.

In front of him, he watched as the cars hovered just slightly off the roads. But the roads weren't paved; instead, they were made of a smooth, whitish material that hummed as vehicles passed over it. The curbs had raised edges with bright orange paint on them, presumably to show where the road stopped and started.

Zac approached it and tried to step off, but there was some kind of invisible barrier preventing him from simply walking onto the street, whatever it was.

The buildings stretched high into the sky, more massive than any he had seen back in his own time. A huge metropolis spread before them; it looked pristine and immaculate. Nothing was dirty. It was as if the sidewalk had never been touched by anything.

Several cars sped by, and Zac marveled at how similar they were to vehicles in his own time, but they were only slightly modified on the exterior. He could only guess at what kinds of technology was on the inside.

Even the sky was a brilliant blue; any pollution had long since been cleaned up. Maybe that was because these vehicles didn't seem to run on gasoline, he reasoned. It had something to do with the street itself.

"Amazing," Emilee said. "Brilliant, really."

"What?" Zac asked.

She pointed to the cars. "I think they're maglev. Magnetic levitation. Back in our time, they use it for some high-speed trains, but to use it for the road system..." Her mouth dropped open in awe. "That makes so much sense."

Zac thought of the hospital bed that seemed to hover in mid-air. Maybe it, too, used magnetic fields to move. He took out the Wand and looked at it. The device still only had one light on it that was lit. "Do you think all this magnetism could be affecting the Wand?" he asked.

"Maybe," Emilee shrugged. I don't know how strong the magnetic field is here. Their technology here might be adapted to it, but maybe it's causing the Wand to malfunction."

Zac grabbed Emilee's hand and pressed down on the top of the Wand. "Nope," he said. "Nothing yet." He put the Wand back in his pocket. "We should get out of here, try to find someplace further away from the city if we can. At least someplace where the magnetism isn't as strong. We don't even know how much power the device has left."

"But we don't even know where we are," Emilee said.

"I think it's our own city," Zac said. "Just a hundred and fifty years in the future. These streets look familiar, even with all the huge skyscrapers."

"I hope you're right," Emilee said. "We need to move fast."

Zac stared at the wall on the outside of the hospital, which was now flashing another image. The same picture of Emilee was projected, but under it, the words had changed. Instead of saying "Considered Dangerous," it flashed the words "Unauthorized Exit—Retrieval Units Tracking."

"Retrieval Units?" Emilee asked. "What could those be?"

Zac stared through the door of the hospital, watching as the security guard at the desk looked up from his monitor and pointed at them.

"I think we're about to find out," he said. "Run!"

TWENTY

Zac grabbed Emilee by the hand and took off down the street, moving as fast as he could. He didn't want to stop and look back to see who was following him. It didn't matter; all he had to do was get them far enough away so that he could activate the Wand.

He checked its light status; still only one light. They tried the Wand again, but nothing happened. They had to find a way to get farther from the road, from these buildings that used a stronger magnetic field.

Then a thought filled him with dread. He didn't even know if there *would* be a place in the future that didn't have the same kind of magnetic field.

They kept running, coming upon a small arch-like structure. People stood on top of it, looking down. "There," Zac said, grabbing Emilee by the arm. "I think we can hide under there. It looks like a bridge or something."

They ran under it, following the pathway. The sidewalks were so different that it was hard to get used to walking on something other than concrete. This was more like a thick plastic, sort of like Plexiglas. Once under the bridge, he leaned against the wall.

"Let me see your Wand," he said. Emilee held it out for him to see. "What happened to it?" he asked. "Did you break it?"

"No; do you think I would be that stupid?"

"No, but I'm just completely confused about how you got here. Bryce said you two talked last night about what I did, and then you got to talking about your past, and —"
"Wait," Emilee interrupted, "what do you know about *my* past?"

Zac froze. He wasn't supposed to let her know that he knew. "I just know you had a rough start," he said. "Bryce told me that things were pretty bad for you growing up, and that of all people, you'd be the one who would want to change it."

She rolled her eyes and paced back and forth. "I told him that in confidence." She fumed. "That's nobody's business."

"I won't tell anyone," Zac said, almost as an apology. "I know you don't want anyone to know."

"That's not the point," Emilee said. "I don't really care if you know; you're not the type of person to take pity on me. I know my stepfather was a horrible person. I just don't want people seeing *me* through a different lens." She stopped. "So that's why you've been asking me all these questions, haven't you?"

"I'm sorry?" Zac said.

"You think I used TEMPUS to get rid of my stepfather, don't you?" Zac didn't answer. "I can't believe you'd think such a thing about me. I know we're just starting to get to know each other, but I'd like to think that you'd give me more credit than *that*." She sighed. "I know the rules. I would never try and change anything."

"Sorry," Zac said, hanging his head. "Bryce told me it was bad, so I figured…"

"Oh, it was bad, all right. You have no idea how many black eyes and bruises I got trying to keep the bastard from hitting my little brother. I've thrown myself in front of his belt more times than I could count when he came in drunk and looking for a fight. But no matter what he did to me, no matter how much I had to lie to the teachers at school, saying that I sprained my hand on something, I never let him win. He never had the satisfaction of defeating me deep down."

Zac started to say something, but stopped himself.

"So, yes, Zac, I was abused. I wish it didn't happen, but it did. And I would never go back in time and try to stop it from happening to me, and you know why?" Zac shook his head. "Because I stood up to him and never let him win. I kept him from hitting my little brother and that means *I won*. I was stronger than him; I *am* stronger than him. It's what made me who I am today. Now, *no one* will ever be able to destroy my willpower."

Zac simply stared at the ground, unsure of what to say. How could he argue with her? She had endured more than he would ever want to. Not just physically, but emotionally and psychologically. Yet the past made her into the person she was today. How would he be different if his mom hadn't died? Would he be better? Worse?

"I'm sorry," he said. "I didn't realize."

"Shh!" she said. She held up her hand, listening. "Do you hear something?"

Zac froze. "Maybe someone's coming down the sidewalk."

She shook her head, concentrating. "It was more of a metallic sound. Like a scraping, but light."

Zac shrugged. "I say we keep going. I think we lost anyone that was following us."

With a flash of movement, something silver moved across the ground toward Emilee. Zac couldn't make out what it was before it had wrapped around her legs, bringing her to the ground.

It was thin and made of several metal plates, each one interlocking like scales. The machine resembled a large snake about six feet long and about two inches in diameter, just slightly thicker than a jump rope. At its "head" Zac could see a small, blinking green light.

"Get it off me!" Emilee screamed. "What is this thing?"

Zac could hear voices in the distance getting closer. "It stopped moving," the voice said. "I think it's tracked the target."

Emilee tried prying the coils away from her legs, but each time she moved, it tightened, constricting until she cried out in pain.

Zac struggled with it, pulling its head away while trying to find a way to push it to the ground. Whatever this thing was, it was tough. "Roll over," he said.

"What?!"

"Roll over so I can move the head next to the ground. I can try to smash it or something."

Emilee squirmed as she moved to her side, the head of the serpent-like object against the ground. Zac raised his foot and began stomping it, but it was resilient. The voices got closer.

"The boa's got something," a voice said. "It's not going anywhere."

"I have an idea," Zac said. "Give me your Wand."

"What?" Emilee said. "It's broken. The middle's crushed."

"Yeah, that's what I'm counting on," he said. "It's just crushed; it doesn't look like it's completely broken open like when the dinosaurs bit into mine. Maybe there's still some energy left in it."

"Just hurry," Emilee said, clenching her teeth from the pain.

Zac took the Wand, lifted it high, and slammed it against the machine, right next to the flashing green light. Nothing happened.

The end of the snake opened like a mouth, stiff and rigid, and two sharp daggers protruded like fangs.

Zac shoved the Wand into the opening and stomped hard onto it, collapsing it. A bright flash filled the air accompanied by a small *pop*!

The snake-like machine went limp. Emilee wiggled her legs free and pulled them out from the coils. "Good thinking," she said.

"It was worth a try," he said. "If it didn't work, I was out of ideas." He pulled her to her feet, and she rubbed them.

"Ow," she said, rubbing a sore spot on her right leg.

"What?"

She pulled her pants leg back. There was a small incision made above her ankle. "That's strange. It looks like a surgical cut." She pushed down on it and looked at it curiously. "There's something under my skin," she said. She met eyes with Zac. "I think they did something to me."

They heard a voice. "The boa went off line. Let's get down there and check it."

"They're right above us," Zac said. "We're going to have to make another run for it. Can you do that?" Emilee nodded.

Zac grabbed the broken Wand, and they dashed out the other side where the sidewalk exited, looking behind them to see several shadows descending into the space under the bridge. Zac could see a man pick up the body of the mechanical snake, holding it limply and dropping it.

Ahead, the space opened up, and there were fewer buildings. It was a park or something. They rushed to it, and Emilee called to Zac. "Wait," she said. "My leg is really starting to kill me now." She was hopping on one foot, scratching at the spot she had discovered.

She looked behind her and walked over to a bench, sitting down. "I don't know what this is," she said.

Zac sat down next to her and examined her ankle. "It's small," he said. "I can see it beneath your skin right now. Sort of a grayish mark." He pressed his finger to it, and he could move it back and forth. "Does that hurt?"

Emilee shook her head. "No."

Zac glanced around to see if they were being followed. Something in the distance glinted in the sunlight, somewhere near the area around the walking bridge they had come from. He took a deep breath and checked the indicator on the Wand. It had two lights now. His theory seemed to be correct; something with the maglev streets might be interfering with it. They had to keep moving.

"What's that?" Emilee asked. She pointed to a red, round structure in the middle of the park. It was the size of a one-story house. They walked toward it. As they approached, they noticed an engraving toward the center of the object. It was almost like a dome, but had a more rounded bottom. "There's writing here," Emilee said. "It says this building was erected to display the artifacts of the early twenty-first century."

Zac moved in and began reading the ornate text. "Inside, visitors can view the contents of a time capsule that was buried, as well as learn more about the early twenty-first century." He turned to Emilee.

"Let's go inside and see," she replied and stood next to the building. Two large doors parted and slid into the walls, and the two of them stepped inside. The structure was one massive room, the round walls covered with artifacts from Zac and Emilee's time. No one else was inside the mini-museum.

Zac smiled as he looked at each item. Some of them were references to movies and music; some were newspaper clippings that were displayed and framed. Each object on the brilliant white walls had a small white space next to it, illuminating a spot on the wall.

Zac touched one, and a video of a person popped up and began narrating, describing popular movies and showing clips of them. "These films were produced using archaic techniques," it said, "and were made before sensory films became the standard format."

Emilee moved along the walls, pressing them and listening to the description of each item as if she had never seen them before. "It's funny," she said. "I never would have thought something like a cell phone would one day seem like an ancient relic."

Zac moved to a spot on the wall opposite her. It was a single white screen surrounded by a black space on the wall. It stood in total contrast to the rest of the walls. Zac and Emilee stared at it, and Zac reached out to touch the wall. The video began.

"In the early twenty-second century, an earthquake caused untold damage to the city, unearthing a forgotten time capsule right under this very location. The capsule's marker had been missing, but the capsule itself contained items from the early twenty-first century. Each item has been researched and is displayed here. Touch the wall next to an item to hear more about it."

Zac continued looking throughout the room. "For a city demolished by an earthquake, they cleaned it up pretty well."

Emilee stopped. "Zac, come here. Look at this. Isn't this... you?"

Zac hurried over to where Emilee was standing. Behind a glass panel, mounted on the wall, was the picture he had put in the time capsule.

"That means... this is right where our old high school used to be..."

"That's you, isn't it? With your mom and dad when you were little?"

Zac nodded, a tear filling his eye. He blinked it away. He didn't want Emilee to see him so emotional. Time had flown past, he thought. He was no longer the scraggly-haired kid in the picture, arms wrapped around his dad's neck. He was so happy back then. Both of them were. Zac pressed the illuminated spot on the wall next to the picture to hear what it said.

"This photograph was included by a student named Isaac R. It is assumed that this is simply a family picture and nothing of significance."

"Nothing of significance?" Zac said. "That's the last picture I have of my mom."

Emilee put her hand on his shoulder. "Let's get going," she said. "We shouldn't stay here too long." She grabbed him by the elbow and moved him along.

"Wait," he said, stopping. On the wall was a piece of writing; the penmanship looked familiar. "I think that's what my dad had me put in the time capsule for him." He approached it with caution, not sure if he should be reading it. His dad told him it was something for people in the future who would be ready for what he had to say. But he'd probably never have this chance again. He had to know what his dad had asked him to put in the capsule. He stepped forward and began to read out loud.

"I have made a great many mistakes in my life. I have made a great many discoveries as well. As a scientist, I've embraced the possibilities, and have found that some lead to great success, whereas others lead to failure. I confess that my second greatest accomplishment in life, the TEMPUS Project, was tempered with loss and sadness. In an effort to understand the past, I had to come face to face with the fact that I could not change it. Changing it would not allow me to create TEMPUS. My son and I have grown apart as a result of my discoveries, for I cannot communicate to him how inextricably our past and my present work are woven together.

I will never be able to tell him, and although I would give anything to change the past misfortune that has befallen us, I cannot. My loving wife of twelve years would not want me to, knowing what I have accomplished. However, I am reminded every time I look at my son that although TEMPUS has been used to cause great good, it comes with great sorrow."

Zac looked at Emilee, who seemed just as perplexed. "What does he mean?" she asked. "I've never heard him talk about this."

"I don't know," Zac said. He continued reading. "In this time capsule, I wish not only to leave a confession of my greatest shortcoming, but also a record of my greatest accomplishment to be preserved throughout history." Below it was a picture of Zac with his mom and dad. "My family is, and always will be, the best thing I've ever done with my life. I only regret that I have not had the courage to tell my son. Perhaps someday I will overcome my inadequacies and will let him know."

It was signed by his dad, and even though Zac could read the handwriting, he knew most people wouldn't be able to discern it.

"Do you want to hear what they have to say about it?" Emilee asked, reaching toward the wall.

Zac stopped her hand and guided it back to her side. "No," he said. "I don't think what they say matters." He smiled to himself and walked out the door.

Outside, the sun was starting to go down, its golden light reflecting off the towering buildings. How long had they been in there?

They tried the Wand again; nothing.

"Wait a minute," Emilee said. "Your dad can help us."

"What?" Zac asked, moving ahead.

"If we're in the same city as where we live, but just in the future, then that means that the TEMPUS building might still be here."

"But my dad would be long gone by now," Zac said. "He *can't* help us."

"No, but whoever is carrying on his work *could*," she said. "They probably have the technology to send us back even if your Wand doesn't work again. It's our best hope."

"I don't have a better idea," Zac said. "Let's head toward it and see what we can find."

There was a clicking sound that came from the grass and Emilee froze. "Did you hear something?"

Zac stopped and listened. "Nothing," he said. "Probably just your imagination." He walked on.

Emilee followed, her steps faster and lighter. She felt something slam against her ankle and yelled out.

"What?" Zac said, and turned to see her.

Emilee lay on the ground, her legs wrapped to her knees with a coiled metallic creature. Before she could let out a scream, it opened its mouth, revealing two needle-like structures that protruded from it. The boa clamped down onto her thigh, the needles digging into her flesh.

TWENTY ONE

The boa withdrew its long needles, retracting them into its mouth and closing it. It squeezed Emilee's legs, and she let out a yelp of pain. Small spots of blood soaked her jeans where the needles had been.

"What do we do?" she said. "I can't even move." Panic spread across her face, her look pleading with Zac to do something.

Zac grabbed the boa's sleek, plated metal body. He tugged at its coils, but they were fixed; every time he pulled against them he was met with a resistance that squeezed even tighter. Emilee winced in pain, and Zac stopped. The last time, all it took was the energy from Emilee's broken Wand to destroy it. He wasn't about to use his own Wand to try to escape.

He struggled against the machine as it held on with its iron grip. Emilee's legs were pinned, and soon the people who were tracking them would arrive and take them away. If that happened, they might never get home.

An idea struck Zac. Emilee had said it felt like there was something in her skin above her ankle, something that was *put* there. Maybe it was a type of tracking device. Maybe it was implanted in her when she showed up at the hospital as an unknown person.

The boa remained motionless; it was no longer fighting them.

"Zac, I'm starting to feel… strange," Emilee said. A sleepy look fell over her, her eyes growing dim.

"Stay with me," Zac said. "I think I know what that thing in your skin is. Some sort of microchip or something they're using to follow you."

"Huh?" Emilee asked. She was slipping now. The machine must've injected her with some sort of sedative to slow her down. He had to do something fast.

"I'm going to have to do something that might hurt," he said. "Do you trust me?"

She nodded, grogginess overtaking her.

Zac searched the ground for something he could use. He walked back and forth through the grass, peering down to see if there was anything he could use. He came to the sidewalk and stopped. The thick, plastic-like material was cracked along one edge that met the grass. It looked like a piece of it was chipping away. He reached down and touched it with his fingers, wiggling a shard that was splitting off. He moved it back and forth until it broke off.

Emilee was drowsy now, her body relaxing as the injection took effect. Whoever was following them would be here soon.

Zac knelt down next to her feet. "You ready?" he asked. Emilee didn't answer; he couldn't tell if she could even hear him. He placed the sharpest tip of the shard against her skin, right next to the incision that was on her ankle. He closed his eyes and took a deep breath, then with a fast slicing motion, slid the shard against it.

Emilee sat up and screamed; the boa tightened again. Clearly, whatever she was injected with hadn't gone all the way through her system yet.

"This might hurt," Zac said. "Don't watch." He dug the plastic-like splinter into the cut and wiggled it back and forth, scraping it against her ankle as he tried to pry out the small gray object.

Emilee squeezed her eyes shut as she turned her head away. A tear ran down her cheek, and she gritted her teeth in pain, trying not to scream out.

"Got it!" Zac said, and held up a tiny, square piece of metal. "I don't know what it is, but I'm getting rid of it." He tossed it into the grass, far off in the distance.

Immediately, the boa released its grip and slithered after it. Emilee breathed a sigh of relief as she relaxed her legs.

"That's how it knew," she said. "But why are they following me? It's not like I'm a wanted criminal or anything."

"I don't know," Zac said, wiping the blood on the grass. "Maybe it's just some kind of way they identify people in the future. Let's not wait around to find out." He stood up and raised Emilee to her feet. She stumbled, and he caught her by the arm. "You gonna be okay?"

She shook her head. "I'm just a little dizzy, that's all. I think whatever they put in me is still spreading." She draped her arm over Zac's shoulder and steadied herself on him. "We need to keep moving. It's not too far from here."

They walked on, putting more distance between themselves and the park. Every few minutes, Zac checked the Wand to see if it would work, but it didn't, even though there were more lights. The Wand was up to three now; apparently there was less interference.

Zac talked continually to Emilee, asking her questions to keep her lucid. "Stay with me," he said. "TEMPUS is just ahead if my sense of direction is right."

They arrived at a flat surface, a metal platform that was surrounded by concrete on all sides. Zac relaxed, surveying the area. Something was wrong.

"I don't get it," he said.

"What?" Emilee asked. She was getting weaker. The cut on her ankle was causing her more discomfort, and she continued to limp.

"This is where TEMPUS was… where it should be." He turned completely around, looking in all directions. "It's gone."

"Are you sure this is the right place?" Emilee asked, her speech slightly slurring.

"Yes," Zac replied. "The cemetery's over there." He pointed to the distance, the green grass engulfing gravestones and surrounded by a bright white fence. It looked like it was made from the same material as the sidewalks. "My dad had the TEMPUS headquarters built here so he could always see my mom's grave from his office."

He lowered Emilee and sat down, taking a rest. He brought his legs up to his chest and wrapped his arms around them, resting his forehead against his knees. "We're trapped here," he said. "We'll never get home."

"We might," Emilee said. "You'll figure something out." She relaxed her eyes.

"Me? I don't have any idea what to do. This place is abandoned; it's like it was filled in with concrete or covered in metal or something. Why would they do that?"

Emilee struggled to speak. "Maybe… maybe people found out that time travel wasn't such a great idea after all. Maybe it was too much of a temptation to change things that weren't meant to be changed."

"But wouldn't anything they changed affect us, too?"

Emilee didn't answer but was still breathing. Zac glanced at the cemetery in the distance. He stood up and lifted Emilee with him, guiding her toward his mother's gravestone.

"What are we doing?" Emilee asked.

Zac was quiet. "We have no place else to go, no one we can turn to. We're out of options and I don't know what to do." They approached the gateway and followed the sidewalk into the small, ancient space. The gravestones were aged, some more than two hundred years old, crumbling away from the cruelty of time. Zac made his way down the sidewalk toward the familiar space, the place he had visited so often.

Even nearly two centuries later, it was the one place that felt like it hadn't changed to him. His mother's gravestone was just ahead; he could pick it out among a sea of monuments just like it.

"My dad doesn't talk about it," he told Emilee. He wasn't sure why he was telling her about it. Maybe it was to keep her alert. Maybe he just wanted to keep himself from crying. "The way she died in front of us... I hope I never have to witness anything like that ever again." He looked at Emilee, who was trying her best to listen and keep her eyes open. "It was in a crowded place. I've asked my dad about it, but he refuses to tell me more. He says he doesn't remember anything, but I know he remembers it. He just doesn't want to."

They reached the place his mom was buried. It was almost a holy place for him, the one place he felt most connected to her. Even now, he felt like she was right there with him, watching over and guiding him.

He lowered himself down and placed his fingertips on the gravestone, running his fingers across the worn letters of his mom's name. It was something he did each time he visited it. It gave him a sort of physical connection to her. Though worn with time, it was still legible.

"They never caught the person who did it. Even with all those witnesses there."

Zac recoiled his hand as he looked to the left of her name. Something else was carved there. He rubbed away the dirt covering it to reveal his dad's name. He had forgotten that his parents planned on being buried next to each other. He froze as he saw the date of his dad's death.

It was the same date as when he had used TEMPUS to find Emilee.

TWENTY TWO

Zac shook his head and read the date again. It couldn't be true. That would mean that his dad would die today. That is, the today of the present, Zac's present.

Somehow, on the same day he used the wormhole to bring him here, his dad died.

Or was killed.

Maybe TEMPUS wasn't malfunctioning. Maybe Emilee didn't come here by accident. Could it be possible that none of this was a coincidence, that someone had orchestrated it this way? A chill ran up his spine. He had to get back to his own time.

"Emilee," he said, gently shaking her. "Emilee, we need to get going. Something's gone wrong."

"Hmmm?" she mumbled, barely awake.

"I think someone brought you here as a distraction. I think someone else was behind sending us to prehistoric times when we tried to go to Roswell." Emilee stirred. "I'm starting to think that someone *wanted* us to think that TEMPUS was malfunctioning."

"Why?" she asked. She was almost completely passed out now.

"I don't know. But if we don't get back to stop them, it means my dad is going to die." Zac took the Wand and checked the indicator lights. Only three were lit up. Was there still interference? Or did it mean that it was losing power? Zac didn't want to wait to find out. He could walk around all day trying to make all four lights show, but if it was losing power, that might not happen.

He put his hand under Emilee's chin, lifting her face and looking into her eyes. He spoke in a soothing voice, calm and yet urgent. She tried to open her eyelids but could barely lift them.

"Emilee," he said, "I'm going to try to get us back. We're going to have to try to go back like we did when you held on to me and used your Wand." He lifted her up, and her head flopped down onto his shoulder, her arms hanging limply at his sides. "I don't expect it to work, but I'm going to try again." He wrapped his arms around her waist and pulled her close.

Zac gripped the Wand and placed his thumb on the sensor. "Here goes nothing," he whispered, and shut his eyes, pressing down hard.

He felt like he was thrown back, like something had slammed into him. He could still feel Emilee next to him and clung to her. His teeth hurt, and a throbbing pain like a migraine pulsed through his head. His muscles tensed, and it felt like his arms were being stretched out of his shoulder sockets.

And then, nothing.

Zac felt a cold, smooth surface under him. Emilee lay next to him, eyes still closed. He leaned in and checked to see that she was still breathing; she was.

He sat up, looking through the glass that surrounded the platform. He breathed a sigh of relief, realizing that they were back. He gently shook Emilee, trying to wake her. She stirred and sat up, taking in her surroundings.

"Where are we?" she asked, blinking her eyes. She seemed confused and frightened at the same time.

"We're back," Zac said. "At least, I think we are." He helped her to her feet, draping her arm around him. "I'm going to take you up and help you find a place to rest. It looks like the sedative is wearing off. I need to find my dad." He led her toward the hallway but stopped when he heard a voice behind him.

"Is everything okay?" Bryce came running over and grabbed Emilee's other arm, steadying her.

"I can walk on my own," Emilee said in a labored voice. "You guys don't have to help me." She tried taking a step without them, but stumbled under her own weight.

"She's hurt," Zac said with urgency.

"I'm fine," Emilee insisted.

"No," Zac said, "that thing bit you or injected you or whatever it did. You need to get it looked at."

"What thing?" Bryce asked, examining the small spots of blood soaking through her jeans. "What happened?"

They guided Emilee up the hall toward the office. "Emilee didn't use TEMPUS," Zac said. "Someone else did, and they left her in the future with a broken Wand so she wouldn't be able to get back."

Bryce stopped. "Who?" he asked Emilee.

"She doesn't know," Zac answered for her. "She said someone took her and she doesn't remember anything. When I found her, she was in a hospital. I need to talk to my dad, right now."

Bryce nodded. "Yeah, I'll take Emilee and have her checked out."

"I don't *need* to be checked out," she protested. "I just want to rest a little. Just let me lie on the couch for a while. I'm already feeling better." Zac could tell the sedative wasn't affecting her as much anymore; she was much more alert.

"Fine," Bryce said. "I'll take you. Zac, I think your dad is in his office."

"Wait," Emilee said. She grabbed his hand, and Zac turned to face her. Emilee leaned in and gently kissed him on the cheek. "Thanks," she said. "For coming after me." She smiled. "And for not leaving me." She gave his hand a small squeeze and let go.

Zac's mind swirled as Emilee and Bryce turned and walked down the hallway. He brought himself back to his senses and hurried to his dad's office. What would Zac tell him? He couldn't tell him about the date on the gravestone. He needed to tell him that TEMPUS was being tampered with. Someone was behind it all. Someone that wanted to see it shut down for one reason or another.

He threw open the door to his dad's office. Dr. Ryger looked up in surprise.

"Zac," he said. "What do you need?" His mood changed to anger.

"Dad," he said, "I need to talk to you about TEMPUS. I think something's wrong."

"I know there is," his dad said. "That's why I shut it down, but you still went and disobeyed me, activating it again. Right now, I'm considering having Chen and Bryce removed from the project for what they did."

"I'm sorry," Zac said. "I know I shouldn't have used it, but I needed to do something about the attack. I couldn't just sit back and watch."

"Yes, you *could* have," his dad said. "But instead, you risked everything because of your impatience."

"That doesn't matter now," Zac said. "Dad, I need you to listen to me. Something bad happened. Someone close to the project wants TEMPUS to fail; they want *you* to fail."

"It *does* matter!" his dad yelled. "You don't just go and decide to travel through time at your own whim! There are consequences!" His tone softened. "Look at Rock; look at his brother. I don't want the same thing happening to you or to anyone else."

"But it *did* happen to someone else, Dad. It happened to Emilee."

"What?"

"She disappeared. At first, we thought she had gone back to change things in her past, but when I found her, she was in the future."

Dr. Ryger looked stunned. "The future? But we never travel to the future. No one should ever know what will happen to them. It might guide their future choices."

Zac thought of the date he saw on the gravestone. What if it wasn't true? What if that was just one possibility? By coming back to save his dad and making sure he was okay, did he change things? "I don't want to argue, Dad," he finally said. "But Emilee didn't use TEMPUS; someone abducted her and used it to take her to the future."

"But that's impossible. There are only a handful of people who know about that computer system, and Emilee is the one who helped design the program for it. No one else understands the programming code."

Zac was about to reply, but he stopped himself. A sudden realization filled him with dread. Emilee was the one who had programmed the computer, but there was more than one person who knew how to operate it. She wasn't the only one who knew how to set the coordinates for the wormhole.

"Dad," Zac said, "where's Chen right now?"

"I sent him home," Dr. Ryger said.

Zac backed out of the room. "I need to get back down to the platform," he said. "I think I know who messed with TEMPUS and manipulated the wormhole."

TWENTY THREE

The underground chamber was empty when Zac entered. He moved past the glowing pentagon and around the corner, heading straight toward the computer. Maybe he could discover some kind of evidence that would show him how Chen caused TEMPUS to malfunction and send them to the wrong time period.

When Zac came to the computer, Bryce was already there, typing at the keyboard. He looked up at Zac. "Hey," he said.

"I think I know what's been happening," Zac told him. "I need you to help me get some information from the system."

Bryce pushed himself away from the screen, rolling back in his chair. "I can't right now. Maybe after I get back." He got up and started walking around the corner.

"When you get back?"

"Yeah. I got all the information I need. I think I've got it figured out."

Zac pressed him for answers. "What information? You know what's going on, too?"

Bryce smiled. "I know what I need to do to end all this."

"What do you mean?"

Bryce continued walking toward the pentagon. It hummed louder, and the glass door swung open.

"It's better if you don't know. But soon, I'll put everything right." He patted Zac on the shoulder. As he turned around, Zac noticed something. Tucked into Bryce's pants at his waist was a gun.

"Is that...?"

"Yeah," Bryce said solemnly. "I'm afraid so." It was like it didn't even affect him, like it was totally normal to be carrying around a gun.

"You can't go killing anyone!" Zac said. "We can still stop Chen without killing him. We just need to find him."

Bryce stood near the platform. "Chen? I'm not going after Chen."

"What are you doing then?"

Bryce sighed as he paced back and forth in front of the machine. "Let me ask you something, Zac. Is it easy knowing that you can travel through time, and yet you can't do anything to save your own mother even though you know it would make your life better?"

Zac frowned. "Of course," he said. "I wish I could, but it's not possible."

"What if it was?"

Zac stared at him, confused. "But it's not. I get that now."

Bryce shook his head. "So I see you've swallowed that line of bull too, huh? Can't change the past... it'll cause a wound in time?" He laughed to himself. "We can't change it, yet we can view it, even if that means watching someone you love die over and over again."

Zac was at a loss for words. Bryce looked so hurt right then; Zac could hear it in his voice. "I know how hard it is to watch your mom die."

"You have *no idea!*" Bryce yelled, slamming his fist against the glass. It shook from the impact. "You've only seen your mom die once. Try watching it again and again."

"But—"

"And *then* try watching it while knowing there's nothing you can do, nothing you can change. Try living with it appearing in your nightmares every night, never knowing what's real and what's in your head. Were those real bursts of heat you felt when the planes hit the towers? Or was it something your mind put there? Do you have any idea what that does to someone?"

"No, but I can guess. I already told how I had that dream about the subway train," Zac replied.

"That was one event," Bryce said. "It doesn't get any easier. And then you start questioning it all. I mean, do you really think the information you gave the authorities will help them stop the terrorists? How do you know our interference isn't paving the way for someone or something worse?"

"I have to believe that we're doing some good, that eventually they'll catch the guys who blew up that subway. Think of all the good you've accomplished on past missions. I know you're upset, Bryce, but you can get help."

"I don't need help," Bryce said. "I told you, I figured out how to fix all this. I won't have to worry about seeing my mom die anymore." He stepped into the pentagon.

"But you can't stop what happened. You can't save her."

"I'm not going to," he said, raising his Wand. "I'm going to save *myself*. I'm going to make sure that I never have to witness it again. I'm going to make sure that I'll never see it more than once." Anger spread across his face. It was like he had become a different

193

person: bitter, vengeful, destructive. "If your dad never discovers how to build this stupid time machine, I'll never have to worry about seeing her die over and over."

"But that won't work," Zac said. "It's already been built. You can't stop it from being built because you'll be *using* the machine to go back and stop him."

"That's just your dad's worthless theory," he said. "I believe that I *can* change it, and the effects will eventually trickle down through history. It's the only chance I've got." He wiped his eyes. "If it works, then none of this will even matter. TEMPUS will never be built, you and I will never have met, and all of the pain you and I have gone through, knowing what we do, helpless to change things… it will all be gone."

"Bryce, come on," Zac pleaded. "Come out from there. Maybe my dad can help you work things out. You don't even know when he built the machine."

"No," Bryce said, shaking his head, "but I have a good idea when it was. When your dad had Emilee program TEMPUS, he made sure one specific date was blocked out so that no one could travel to it. I think he's protecting that date. When I abducted Emilee and took her to the future, I only did it to get the information I needed from her, to learn how to unblock the date. I figured if I could leave her at that hospital in the future, there'd be no way for her to get back and stop me. They'd think she was crazy, rambling on about being from a different time period."

"But then why did you let me use TEMPUS to get her?" Zac asked.

"I thought it would be a convenient way to get you out of the picture, too. At least until I had accomplished what I intended to. I never actually expected you to get past their security units and to come back with her."

Zac tried to speak but could not find the words to say.

"I've got to get going," Bryce said as the door closed. He held out the Wand. "And Zac, please know that I'm sorry. I'm only doing what's best for everyone. If you have anything you want to say to your dad, I'd go do it now. You don't have much time left with him."

Bryce pressed the sensor on the Wand and disappeared in an undulating wave of blue energy.

Zac ran into the conference room and shook Emilee. "I need your help," he said. "Bryce is gone."

"Huh?" Emilee said, waking up. "Yeah, I know. He went home after bringing me here."

"No," Zac said, shaking his head. "It was him. He used TEMPUS. He's the one who abducted you."

Emilee sat up, rubbing her eyes. "Wait a minute. What are you talking about?"

"He's upset," Zac said, talking a mile a minute. He stood and began walking back and forth. "He's angry at not being able to do anything. He said he doesn't want to have to watch his mom die over and over."

"His mom?"

"The planes," Zac said. "She was in one that hit the World Trade Center towers."

Emilee raised her hand to her mouth. "Oh, God... I had no idea. But he..."

"Yeah, I know. He acted like he was okay with it, but deep down it was tearing him apart. He said he was going to go back and change things. He said you gave him a way to access a date that my dad classified as restricted."

Emilee furrowed her brow. "I never gave him any information."

"That's not what he says. He said he got it from you when he abducted you. You said you passed out when that happened, right?"

Emilee thought for a moment. "Yeah, I think so," she said. "Do you think he did anything to drug me?"

"Maybe. He said he's going to prevent my dad from creating the time machine. I think he's going to kill him. I need you to tell me what you told him. I need you to help me use TEMPUS to go back and stop him."

"I don't think that's such a good idea," she replied. "He can't do that, can he?"

"Doesn't matter," Zac said. "He's already left. He's going to try. I need to stop him."

Emilee pushed herself off the couch. "Let's just go tell your dad," she said. "He'll be able to think of something."

"No!" Zac said. "He can't know. In the future, the date on the gravestone said he dies today; if he knew what was happening, he would want to go after Bryce by himself to talk some reason into him, but I don't think that's going to happen. Bryce took a gun."

"Oh, God…"

Zac nodded. "Now will you please help me?"

Emilee walked with him down the hallway. "I don't know what I told him," she said. "I think I can figure out where the wormhole took him, though. The program always records the destination, so that way, there's a record of where we've been. It should be able to put you pretty close to where he went."

"Thanks," he said. They went behind the bookcase and down the hallway. The familiar blue glow that once beckoned him, igniting his curiosity, now filled him with fear for his own future. If Bryce was going to kill his dad, when would he do it? Would it be before Zac was born? Would that eliminate him from the timeline? "So what date did my dad make you block out?"

"I don't remember," Emilee said. "It didn't seem significant. It was more of a side note when I was doing the programming. I was working with so many numbers back then, I just forgot about it."

They walked to the computer. "Hurry," Zac said. "I don't know how much time we have. If he succeeded, then maybe the changes are bleeding through right now. There's no way to know."

Emilee typed at the keyboard. "I'm looking," she said. "I'm going as fast as I can." She stared at the screen, her eyes moving back and forth as she examined the lines of code. Finally, she put her finger on the screen. "That's the log of the last time leap," she said. "It doesn't tell the date, though. It just gives coordinates for space, not time. I must have masked it somehow." She looked up at him. "Are you absolutely *sure* you want to take a chance and go?"

"I don't have a choice," Zac said. "He's going to try to kill my dad; I just know it. I can't sit by and let it happen. I've already lost one parent. I don't want to lose the other. If I can keep that date on the gravestone from becoming a reality..." His voice trailed off.

Emilee stared at him for what seemed like a long time. "Okay," she said. "I'll do it, but please be careful." She reached out and took his hand, giving it a little squeeze.

"I will," he said. He stared into her eyes for a few seconds more, looking deeper than he had ever done before. This time, it was like she was letting him in, letting him see a piece of herself. Emilee turned and bent down, setting the coordinates in the computer.

Zac walked to the pentagon and stepped inside the glass enclosure. The door closed behind him. The blue lights increased as the power built, the noise growing louder until it sounded like a loud grinding noise.

Emilee walked up, pressing her hand to the glass. She mouthed the words, "Good luck."

Zac lifted his left hand, matching it up with hers. He closed his eyes, and pressed his thumb to the Wand, activating the time machine.

TWENTY FOUR

As soon as the world stopped spinning around him, Zac tried to get his bearings. He spun around, looking for Bryce. Instead, he saw a house that looked familiar.

It was on a small incline and had steep concrete steps leading to the front door with painted black rails on both sides of the steps. The house was covered in light blue siding with dark blue shutters. Two small evergreen trees stood like sentries on either side of the door.

Looking at the mailbox, Zac immediately knew why he recognized this place. Painted black, its paint chipping away, the mailbox had one word below the address: *Ryger*. It was the house he grew up in when he was little, right before they moved.

That would mean… that would mean that this was a time when his mom was still alive. Chills swept over him at the thought that he might be able to see her again.

He searched for any sign of Bryce, but saw nothing. Where could he be? A sudden thought made him sick to his stomach. What if Bryce had already committed the act? Could he have done it so soon?

Zac shook off the thought and continued searching. He crept around the perimeter of the house, looking behind the bushes that guarded the basement windows, checking for any footprints or other evidence left behind. The windows looked like they were still closed; his family had always kept them locked, so Bryce probably had not gone inside that way. He would have needed to use the door.

Zac came around to the other side, next to the garage. Looking out at the point where he had first arrived, he surveyed the scene once more. Still no Bryce. What if this had all been a distraction, another trick? What if Bryce was somewhere else?

He heard the rustle of leaves and turned just in time to see a fist swinging at his face. He dodged, but fell off balance and rolled onto the ground. Bryce stood over him, glaring.

"So you followed me?" he said, anger filling his voice. "What, Zac? Are you gonna try to stop me?"

Zac pushed himself up, placing his hands on his knees, and stood up straight. "I'm not going to let you do this, Bryce."

"Oh, you're not going to *let* me? You think you'll be able to control me?" He began moving in a menacing circle around Zac, who now stood in the middle of the yard. He stopped, his back to the house. "You know, one thing that I've learned from your dad is that control is all about perception. There is no such thing as fate or destiny. We control our own destiny. I'm just now realizing that, and it's why I've come here."

"But why are you so mad at my dad?" Zac asked. "What has he done that's wrong?"

Bryce was incredulous. "What has he done that's *right*? He's playing God, Zac. He's letting people run around in time. There are certain things man isn't meant to do, certain things he shouldn't know."

"What gives you the right to decide that?" Zac said.

"What gives *him* the right to decide on the rules of time travel? Did you ever ask yourself that? Why should he, of all people, be able to tell us what to do? Has he had to watch your mom's death multiple times? He *says* he never tried to prevent it, but I'm sure he's tried. He probably just never told you."

"Bryce, I agree with you, okay? It was wrong for my dad to mess with time. It was wrong for you to have to watch your mom's final moments without being able to do anything." He took a step closer, and Bryce reached for his gun. Zac held his hands up in defense. "But don't compound your pain by doing something you'll regret."

"Regret? The only thing I regret is listening to him for so long. I know he's not an evil person. But he *is* the cause of this. You know all about cause and effect. Cause: some maniac shoots your mom; effect: you still have trouble coping to this day. Cause: your dad builds a device to travel through time; effect: we have to live with the knowledge that we have the power to do something, yet can do nothing." He shrugged his shoulders. "See? Take away the cause, the effect goes away too."

The garage door began to open, and Bryce turned around. Zac tensed. They could hear voices inside the garage.

"I'm doing us both a favor, Zac," he said. "Trust me. If our paths cross in the future, you'd thank me, but you won't remember any of this. It'll all be erased as soon as I pull the trigger." Bryce gripped the gun and began walking toward the garage.

Immediately, Zac lunged at him, tackling him to the ground. Bryce struggled, trying to throw him off, but Zac got on top of him, flattening Bryce to the ground on his stomach. Bryce struggled to lift the gun, but Zac grabbed his hand and turned the gun to point it directly back at Bryce.

They listened to the voices coming from the garage. Zac could hear his dad talking to his younger self.

"Hurry, Dad! We're going to be late!"

"Settle down, Isaac. We'll get to there in time. The mall's just a mile away; it'll only take us a few minutes to get there. You won't miss any of the movie."

Zac watched with curiosity as the shadows moved across the driveway in front of them. He was so little back then.

"Daniel, he's just excited, that's all." It was his mom's voice. It felt so strange to hear it again, yet it felt like just yesterday since he had heard it last. He wanted to let go of Bryce, run to her, and wrap his arms around her in a giant bear hug, never letting her go. He wanted to say all of the things he never got to say, to tell her how much he loved her and how much he missed her.

The car began backing out of the garage. Zac pulled Bryce back and leaned with him against the side of the house, pinning the hand with the gun to Bryce's chest so he couldn't use it. Looking to his left, Zac watched the car back out of the driveway and into the street. He could see himself sitting in the back of the car. He tried to remember what movie he had seen, but they had gone to the movies so often, it could've been any one. The car drove away, and he felt a little bit of hope leave with it.

Bryce jerked his head back, slamming it into Zac's nose. Zac let out a yelp of pain and grabbed his face. He rolled over onto his back.

Bryce pushed himself away and spun around. He pushed himself up, the gun pointed at Zac.

"Killing me won't fix anything," Zac said. "You're better than this, Bryce." He tried standing up, but Bryce hovered over him.

"I'm not going to kill you," Bryce said. "I don't want to kill anyone, but I don't have a *choice*, Zac. I can't live like this anymore. I need the memories to go away. I have to make them stop. This is the only way."

"You always have a choice," Zac said. "That's the one thing we do have."

"Yeah, well," Bryce said, hesitating, "I'm choosing to fix my future by changing the past. I'm going after them. Don't try to follow me." He turned to go, but then stopped, feeling his pocket and looking down. He turned, staring down at the grass. His eyes fixated on something in front of Zac.

Zac looked at the same spot and saw what had attracted Bryce's attention. Bryce's Wand had fallen out of his pocket and was just a few feet away.

Both of them stared at it, daring the other to make a move. Zac scrambled forward, grabbing the Wand in a sweeping motion. He backed up close to the driveway and held it up for Bryce to see.

"Give it here," Bryce said.

"No. Come back with me."

Bryce shook his head. "I told you, I'm not going to do that." He reached out. "Now give me back the Wand."

Zac raised it high, then brought it down with great force and slammed it onto the concrete. A bright flash shot from the object. "Now mine's the only one," Zac said. "If you want to get back, it's gotta be with me."

Bryce laughed. "Do you think I care? I don't think you get it; I never intended to go back. If it's any consolation, if what I do works, you won't remember this confrontation anyway. Goodbye, Zac." He began walking away.

Zac tried standing up. "Bryce, wai—"

Bryce spun around, running and swinging his foot, kicking Zac hard in the jaw. Zac crumpled to the ground. "I told you not to try following me!" he said. Bryce kicked him in the ribs and then in the side of the head. "I'd love to stay and chat," he said, "but I don't want to be late for when the movie lets out." He kicked Zac once more.

Zac groaned in pain, and everything faded into blackness.

A familiar voice woke Zac. Someone was rocking him back and forth, trying to get him to open his eyes.

"What happened?" the voice asked. "Hey, Zac." A hand tapped against his face. "Wake up."

Zac opened his eyes and peered up at the source of the voice. Staring down at him was Chen. "What… what are you doing here?" He sat up and clutched his side where Bryce had kicked his rib cage. It was sore and felt tender.

"Where's Bryce?" Chen asked.

"Huh? How long have I been out?" He rubbed the side of his head and moved his jaw. For all he knew, he could have been out for just seconds, or it could have been an hour. He was still on the ground next to his old house.

"I have no idea," Chen replied. "All I know is that when Emilee told your dad what was going on, he sent me after you. She told us everything."

Zac sat up. "She told my dad? But I told her I didn't want him to know what I was doing."

Chen turned and looked behind himself. "Well, it's too late for that. Look, all I know is that when I got here, you were passed out. What happened? Did you see Bryce?"

"Yeah," Zac said. "I saw him. He's going after my dad. My parents are taking me—well, the *younger* me—to a movie."

"Then there's still time to stop him. Where are they going?"

"It's too late. Bryce has a head start," Zac said. "He'll get there before we do."

"But they're in a movie," Chen said. "If Bryce was on foot, they'll be there before he is. He'll probably wait to ambush them when it's over. Where's the movie theater?"

Zac tried to think. "There are a few of them, but the one we always went to was at the mall. I think I heard them saying that's where they were going."

"Good. Then that's where we'll go," Chen said, extending his hand to help Zac up. "Think you can run?"

"Definitely," he said.

"Then let's go. We don't have much time."

The mall was crowded when they arrived; a sea of people flowed past the stores like fish swimming with the current. Zac and Chen began searching for any sign of Bryce.

"You see anything?" Chen asked.

"No," Zac said. He was beginning to panic. He hated being around this many people. He felt suffocated, like he was being pressed in on all sides. He wanted to run back outside, to breathe in the fresh air out in the open. But he had to press forward. He had to make sure Bryce didn't succeed.

"Where's the movie theater entrance?" Chen asked.

Zac racked his brain trying to remember. All of the stores brought back so many memories; most of them had gone out of business or moved on by now. But seeing them again, he felt like it was just yesterday that he was here. He closed his eyes, trying to picture the entrance to the theater. The velvet ropes that led to the box office, the movie posters framed along the wall and surrounded by lights... he could even remember specific movie posters he'd walked past as a child.

"Anything?" Chen asked. He looked around impatiently as people passed him, bumping into him. Someone mumbled something about getting out of the way.

"I'm trying," Zac said. "I remember it being upstairs... yeah," he said, nodding. "It opened up right next to an escalator. I remember going up the escalator each time and then seeing the box office."

"Then let's find an escalator," Chen said, and began walking.

Zac followed; they both searched the crowd for any sign of Bryce. He'd probably gotten there earlier, but he didn't know where to look. It probably wouldn't take him long to find out, though.

They wound their way through the crowd, making their way toward the escalator. There were several of them throughout the mall, but Zac was starting to get his bearings back. He stopped at a map kiosk to make sure he was headed in the right direction.

The escalator was just ahead. "Wait," Zac said. "What do we do if we see Bryce? He has a gun. There are too many people here who could get hurt."

Chen sighed. "We have to neutralize him somehow. Get him away from all these people."

Zac thought. "I have an idea," he said. "He doesn't know you're here yet. Let *me* confront him. I'll try to get him to focus on me, and then you can take him from behind. He won't expect it."

Chen considered it. "Okay," he said. "But we have to be careful."

"We will," Zac said. "This has got to work. You need to go somewhere else, someplace he won't see you. If he discovers you're with me, it won't work. Just stay close."

"Will do," Chen said. "Good luck."

"Thanks," Zac said. "And thanks for coming after me to help. I owe you."

Chen smiled. "I'm just surprised you thought *I* was the one who tampered with the machine."

Zac looked down in embarrassment. "Sorry about that," he said. "I didn't think Bryce would do this."

"It doesn't matter right now. Let's just go find him." Chen walked deeper into the crowd, disappearing into the throng of people.

Zac stepped onto the escalator, riding it up while turning to look below. He couldn't see Bryce. He kept his head low so that if Bryce was on the second floor, waiting, he wouldn't spot Zac immediately. Zac wanted to see *him* first.

He glided off the escalator, merging with the people standing in line for tickets. He looked up at the movie times, recalling all the titles of the old films.

He felt someone brush up against him. A voice whispered into his ear. "I told you not to follow me."

"Hi, Bryce," Zac said without turning around.

"You try anything, you say anything, I *will* pull the trigger," he said. "Any minute now, your folks should be walking out of the theater. Now, you can leave calmly, or you can watch me kill him. It's your choice. I don't *want* you to have to watch it. We both know how painful it is to watch a family member die."

Bryce pulled him out of the ticket line and to the side, not letting him turn around. Where was Chen? Did he see them?

"I'm not going anywhere," Zac said. He tried reaching down into his pocket. Maybe if he could grab ahold of Bryce, he could use the Wand and take both of them back to the present. Then Bryce would fail. He tried to be discrete, slowly moving his hand.

Bryce clutched his arm. "What do you think you're doing?" he asked. He squeezed Zac's muscle with an iron grip. Zac winced.

Zac could hear more noise coming from inside the theater lobby. A large group of people came walking out, laughing and talking. A movie had just let out, and people were emptying past the box office and into the mall.

"Looks like the movie's over," Bryce said, "but the real show's just about to start."

TWENTY FIVE

Zac searched the crowd for his parents, for himself. He wanted to yell out or to do something to get everyone's attention, to make it so that Bryce wouldn't be able to act, but he couldn't think straight. Where was Chen?

And then Zac saw them: his parents, walking side by side holding hands. His mom was reaching down, her other hand holding his own.

He wished that his dad didn't look the same as he did in the present. Maybe if he'd looked different, Bryce wouldn't be able to identify him. He silently prayed that Bryce wouldn't notice them, that he might overlook them in the midst of all the people passing by.

He didn't. "Well, here goes nothing," Bryce said. "I hope you said goodbye before you left." He thrust Zac aside and walked toward the family.

"Excuse me, sir. Are you Dr. Ryger?" Bryce asked.

Zac's dad let go of his mom's hand and approached Bryce. "Yes," he said. "Do I know you?"

Bryce smiled. "Not for much longer." He reached into his pocket.

In a blur of motion, Chen rushed in from the side and knocked Bryce to the ground. Dr. Ryger stumbled back in surprise.

Zac rushed in; the gun had fallen from Bryce's grip and had skidded across the floor. He made a dash for it before anyone could see it and grabbed it.

Bryce struggled with Chen, turning around and punching him. Chen tried to resist, but Bryce was stronger. He got up, heading toward Zac, but Chen grabbed his feet and pulled him down, clamping his arms around them.

Zac looked up, clutching the gun. His dad and mom stared at him in horror. He watched as his younger self began cowering and clinging to his mother, crying and frightened.

Bryce struggled, trying to loosen his legs from Chen's grip. One foot slipped out, and Bryce slammed it into Chen's face repeatedly. Chen let go, and Bryce stumbled forward, trying to get up.

Zac had to get his parents out of here. He rushed forward toward them, turning to see how close Bryce was. Chen was standing now, trying to hold him off.

Mall security would be here any minute, but Zac didn't have time to wait. He hurried over to his dad, trying to think of what to say, the words all jumbled in his mind. His heart raced as the adrenaline pumped through his body. He got closer, but his dad backed away from him. He tried to talk, but the words wouldn't come. "Stop!" was all he could manage.

Mass confusion and panic swelled around him as people began to scatter, bumping into each other and screaming.

"Get the hell away!" his dad yelled at him.

Zac approached, confused. His younger self was crying harder now.

"No," he tried saying, "It's okay." He bent down low, trying to talk to the frightened child that was him. "It's okay. Just listen to me."

He heard an angry yell behind him, and Bryce's arm swung around Zac as he tried to grab the gun. Zac held it out, trying to keep it from him.

Relentless, Bryce struggled with him and kept grasping. Zac pushed against him, slipping and falling backward to the ground.

A loud shot rang out, and Zac flinched at the deafening sound. Bryce loosened his grip, and Zac felt himself being yanked backward. Zac stared ahead in shock, watching as his dad hovered over his mother. His younger self stood to the side, holding his hands over his ears and screaming.

Zac tried to stand up but was knocked down as his dad rushed forward, shoving him to the ground. He was filled with rage, and he began pummeling Zac with his fist.

Zac tried to hold up his hand to defend himself, but the blows kept coming.

His younger self began to cry, to plead for his daddy, and Dr. Ryger loosened his grip and rushed over to the child.

Zac tried to get up, backing toward the escalator. He had to get out of here; he had the gun, and he needed to get it away from Bryce. He pulled out the Wand. He stumbled and scooted across the floor, but as soon as he got up and regained his balance, his father turned back around and slammed into him, pushing him down the escalator. The Wand fell from his grip, and Zac tumbled and rolled down the steps, hitting his head and bumping into people. He felt a sharp pain in his neck, and his arm was sliced open by the edge of a step.

He could hear screaming. He felt someone grab him tightly, lifting him up, and then a violent shaking filled his body. The air was sucked out of his lungs, and his chest felt a pressure as if someone was standing on top of him. And then, silence.

Zac crumpled to the ground. He opened his eyes and was greeted by a blue light that enveloped him. He heard the familiar humming sound of the pentagon, and sat up, confused. His whole body ached, and he saw blood running down his arm. He set the gun down on the floor.

He looked behind himself. His dad was there, still holding on to his shoulder and standing up. But it was his dad from the present.

"Dad?" he asked. "What just happened? How are you... how did I get back?"

Dr. Ryger lifted him up and carried him out of the glass enclosure. He rested Zac against the wall. "Just rest," he said, consoling him. "Just rest."

His dad walked around the corner and came back with a bottle of water. He handed it to Zac and sat down next to him.

Zac took a drink and breathed deeply. He was sweating, yet he felt cold in the underground room. Nothing seemed real; he was still in a daze and thought he might be dreaming. He could be having the same kinds of nightmares that Bryce had. Maybe time travel affected the brain that way. Maybe the effects put you in a dreamlike state that felt real.

His dad sighed and patted Zac's leg. Zac took another drink of the ice cold water and allowed it to wash down this throat. He was definitely awake.

"You going to be okay?" his dad asked.

Zac stared at the wormhole chamber, empty except for the pulsating, rhythmic light.

"What happened?" he asked. "Am I crazy, or did I just see what I thought I saw?"

His dad nodded, looking to the side, trying not to make eye contact. "Yeah," he said, "you did."

Zac sat in shock, unable to process what it all meant. Tears filled his eyes, and he managed to whisper. "*I* did it," he said. "It was *me.*"

His dad said nothing but wrapped his arms around his own legs, pulling them to his chest. He looked defeated, like a man who was at the end of his rope.

"Is that how it happened?" Zac asked. "Was it me all along?" Again, he was met with silence.

The answer was obvious, and neither of them wanted to say it. He could still feel the gun recoiling as it went off, could still see his mom double over, could see himself as a child crying desperately, confused. And now, he was just as confused as before, but this time he was overwhelmed with immense guilt. Finally, Zac made himself say the words he dreaded most.

"I'm the one who killed her. It was me that day, wasn't it?" He turned to his dad, who met his gaze.

"Yes," his dad said. "But it wasn't on purpose." Tears began trickling down his cheeks. "You couldn't have known it would happen."

"Is that why you blocked that date from the system?" Zac asked. "Because it was the day she died?"

His father nodded. "I thought that I would block it to protect you, to protect *me* from going back to try and stop the killer. But even though I did everything I could to prevent one of us from going back, it obviously was not meant to be blocked. Her death..." he paused.

Zac shook his head, his voice filled with frustration. He wiped away a tear as he sat against the concrete wall. "No," he said.

"I don't want to hear it. Don't you dare say that she was meant to die." He looked at his dad. "Because that would mean that I was always *meant* to kill her. To kill my own mother." He began sobbing, burying his head inside his sleeve.

Dr. Ryger spoke with tenderness and put his hand on Zac's shoulder. "Son, don't blame yourself. This must have been how it always happened. I always wondered how her death and my finding the Wand device were connected."

Zac looked up. "Wait; where's my Wand?"

"Back there," his dad said. "Back in the past where you dropped it. Back where I found it, where I will pick it up and take it with me. And then I'll notice its peculiar design, and I'll analyze it and realize what it does."

"So that's when you discovered the Wand?"

"Yes," he said, nodding. "I found it that day, and I realized that its design would help me in my research to create a way to travel through time. I was never able to get that one, the original prototype, to work. That is, until you found it."

Zac thought for a moment. "Hang on; what do you mean?"

His dad stood up and started walking back down the hallway toward the computers. Zac got up and followed him. He still ached, but he was slowly slipping out of his shock.

"Here," his dad said, pointing to the small door recessed into the wall, the small compartment where Zac found the Wand the first night he used it. "It wasn't malfunctioning. It was being activated by its original user. You."

Zac ran his hands across the space, remembering the night he found it and stepped near the pentagon. He thought about how the door had automatically opened, inviting him in. How it had taken him back to the date of his birth.

"That means… that means the one I dropped just now and the one I found the first day…" He struggled for a way to frame his thoughts. "Those are the *same?*"

Dr. Ryger nodded. "Yes," he said. "The one you dropped back at the mall is the original. It's the one you took from the case, and it was lost when you were taken back to prehistoric times. That one was destroyed."

"But then you made me a new one, which we activated," Zac said, finally realizing it. "And that one is the one I left behind at the mall. The one which becomes—"

"The original one, the one I had in this case here. That's why it worked for you. *You* were the original owner, so that's why it recognized you when you first discovered it. Because that same Wand would be made for you later. It's a circular paradox."

Zac stood in awe as the machine hummed louder, reverberating throughout the underground cavern. "That's how it's all connected," he said, thinking back to his dad's note from the time capsule. "Without mom's death, you would never discover time travel. But without the ability to travel through time, I would never have gone back to leave the device on accident that day…"

"Do you see now that no matter how much you wished to, you'd never be able to prevent her death?"

The lights flickered. Zac sat down next to the computer, looking at the screen, but not really focusing on it. "Did you know?" he asked.

"Know?"

"That I was the one to kill Mom?"

His dad sighed. "Yes," he said. "Not at first, but I started to wonder after the Wand activated itself when you used it. I wanted to keep you from using it again, but I finally had to face that fact that if it's meant to happen that way, I couldn't do anything to stop it."

Zac said nothing. How could his dad knowingly *allow* him to kill his mom?

"I'm sorry," his dad said, trying to get Zac to face him. "I've been struggling over this since the moment you first used the machine. I haven't been able to eat or sleep much. I worried that every day could be the day that it happened. I desperately wanted to find a way to prevent it. When TEMPUS seemed to be malfunctioning, it gave me hope that I could avoid it; I finally had a reason to shut it down."

"But it still happened..."

"Fate had another plan," he said.

Zac put his head down on the desk. How could "fate" have a plan? Was there no way it could have been avoided?

Zac heard a metallic, clinking sound, and then what sounded like gasping or choking. He lifted his head and turned to see his dad, clutching his throat, sinking to the ground.

Wrapped around his neck was a coil of metal, twitching and squeezing.

TWENTY SIX

Zac watched as his dad crumpled to the ground and knew instantly what was choking him. One of the metallic, serpent-like machines he had seen in the future now gripped his dad's throat, tightening just enough that his dad would have to struggle for air, but not enough that he would pass out.

Zac raced over, trying to pry it loose, realizing that it would be pointless, but attempting to nonetheless. Dr. Ryger raised his hand and motioned for him to stay back; the boa was squeezing a bit tighter every time he touched it. Had it somehow come with him when he brought Emilee back?

A shadow appeared on the floor, spreading over Dr. Ryger's body. Bryce stepped around, smiling and holding something in his hand.

"Amazing things, aren't they?" he said. "I liked them so much I decided to take one with me after I dropped Emilee off." He walked closer. "But you interfered with that. You had to be all brave and go save the day to prove your love for her."

"How'd you get back?" Zac asked. "Your Wand was destroyed."

Bryce laughed. "Yeah, but Chen's wasn't. Luckily, when he used his, he was nice enough to give me a lift back, too." He made a sweeping motion with his hand toward the other room where Chen lay outside the platform. The door was wide open, and Chen lay crumpled in a heap, beaten and bloody.

"Is he…?"

"Dead?" Bryce asked. "No, but he probably wishes he was after what I did to him. Let's just say he won't be getting up for a while."

"Bryce, please," Zac pleaded. "You saw what happened back there. You saw what you made me do. End this."

"Don't you see? That's what I'm *trying* to do!" He lifted Dr. Ryger to his feet. "Now, what you're going to do, Doc, is you're going to reprogram Chen's Wand for *me*." He tossed it to Zac. "And then I'm going to take Zac back with me and make him watch your wife's death again and again. And then I'll take *you* with me, and I'll make *you* watch it over and over too." He gave a smug smile. "I figured that if I couldn't kill you, then maybe I can make it so that you'll actually *want* to find a way to change things. Let's make TEMPUS a nightmare for you like it's been for me."

"He's not going to do it," Zac said.

"Sure he will," Bryce said, holding up the gun. "When you got back, you left this out. Oops." He turned to Dr. Ryger. "Now, that thing around your neck is bad enough, and I'm going to make it tighten a little bit every minute until you do what I say. And if you refuse, I'm going to take away the only thing you have left." He tucked the gun at his side and patted Zac on the back.

Zac swatted his arm away.

218

Dr. Ryger nodded and held up his hand. He stood up, coughing, and lifted himself into the chair in front of the computer. Reaching out, he took the Wand from Zac and typed something into the computer. He turned and gave Zac a knowing glance, motioning with his eyes slightly toward the Wand.

Zac gave him a confused look.

His dad shoved the Wand into Zac's hand and clasped his own hands over Zac's, manipulating his fingers in a strange way. He squeezed Chen's Wand tightly between Zac's fist and nodded, then typed at the keys again.

"Now get it set to take me back so I can watch your wife die," Bryce said, making the mechanical snake tighten more. He grabbed the Wand from Zac and held it, balancing it in the palm of his hand.

Dr. Ryger winced as he pressed the keys, then gave a nod.

"Come say goodbye." He led them to the chamber. "Don't worry; I'll have him home soon." Bryce held up a remote, pressing a button. The mechanical boa fell to the ground, and Zac's dad gulped in a huge breath of air. He nodded to Zac.

"So long," Bryce said, and pressed the top of the Wand. Nothing happened. He looked closely at it; the lights were all lit. He pressed it again.

Zac took this opportunity to elbow Bryce in the face, then spun around behind him and put him in a stranglehold. "Give it up, Bryce." He lowered Bryce to the ground so it would be difficult for him to get up.

Bryce struggled, grabbing at Zac's forearm, trying to pry it away from his neck. He tried to speak but couldn't. "Double-crossed..." was all he could whisper, glaring at Dr. Ryger.

Dr. Ryger approached the platform. "I'm sorry for all the pain I've caused you," he said. "I never meant it to be that way. Let me help you. We can figure something out."

Bryce growled in rage. "No!" he yelled, lurching forward. "It's too late! My life is already ruined!" He began to weep.

"Bryce," Dr. Ryger said, "I can't change the past for you. But everything's going to be okay." He looked to Zac and nodded.

Zac seemed to understand what he needed to do, and pried the Wand from Bryce's grip.

"Now, Zac!" his dad yelled.

Bryce grabbed the gun at his side and raised it, firing at Dr. Ryger. He dropped the gun, and Zac pressed the top of the Wand. The room vanished.

They stood in a small room with pale white walls on all sides. Bryce fell to the ground, gasping. He spun around.

"Where did you take me?" he asked.

"I don't know," Zac said. "I didn't program it; my dad did."

Bryce lunged at him, and he sidestepped, letting Bryce fall to the ground. He shook with sobs and lay there.

"I just wanted to make the pain go away," he said. "I just wanted it to go away." He continued crying as Zac backed away from him.

Zac had no idea where they were, or when, but he knew his dad had programmed it for a reason. He held up the Wand and stepped out of Bryce's reach.

Bryce turned and reached up. "Don't leave me here," Bryce pleaded. "I don't know where this is. Please!"

"I'm sorry," Zac said. "I can't fix what happened to you in the past, but I can keep you from messing with the future." He took a step back. "Goodbye."

"No," Bryce said, getting to his feet. "You can't do this!"

Zac pressed the top of the Wand, and with a ripple of light, vanished from Bryce's sight.

• • •

Zac arrived back in the chamber and stared out from the glass. His father was crumpled against the wall, a blood stain soaking his shirt on his abdomen. Zac stared in horror momentarily, then forced open the shattered door and ran over to him.

"Dad?"

His dad grunted, clutching his stomach.

"Hang in there. I can get you help." He looked over at Chen, who was now stirring. "Chen, can you help? Do something, please!"

Chen was still dazed. He looked over and raised his head, but was too weak to move. He collapsed again.

Zac was frantic. "Dad, I need to run and get you some help. I'll be right back!" He stood to leave but felt a tug on his arm. His dad was looking up at him, his eyes indicating that he wanted to say something. "What?" Zac said, bending down closer.

"… to tell you something…"

Zac tried standing up again. "Tell me when we get help," he said. "Just hang on!"

His dad made a gurgling noise, like he was trying to talk louder but couldn't.

"Stay…" he said. "…time to go…"

Zac shook his head, eyes filling with tears as he understood what his dad was asking him to do. "No," he said. "It's not time yet." His mind's eye flashed to the gravestone he had seen in the future. Today's date.

"…help for Bryce…" he said. "…don't abandon… still hope…"

"Bryce is gone," Zac said. "He can't do anything. Please, Dad, stay with me."

His dad's eyes started to close, but Zac gently shook him. "Dad… Dad?"

Dr. Ryger opened his eyes again. His voice was barely a whisper as the life drained out of him. "… some things… meant to be…"

A silent tear rolled down Zac's cheek, and he sniffed, wiping the tear away. He pulled his dad in close and hugged him.

"…love you, Zac," he said. "Proud of you." He exhaled slowly and within moments, he was gone.

Zac stood over the grave site as the mourners left, each one offering their condolences to Zac and letting him know how sorry they were. Everyone said they knew how he felt, or said they knew it must be hard to lose both parents, but they really had no idea when it boiled down to it.

No one could say they knew how he felt, not really. No one there could say they witnessed both of their parents gunned down in front of their eyes, let alone that they were responsible for one of them. He felt better once everyone started leaving. Only Chen and Emilee stayed behind.

Chen hobbled over on his crutches, his leg in a cast.

"How are you doing?" Zac asked him. Chen's leg was broken, and he had a cracked rib. Bryce had given him a concussion, and he had to be in the hospital for the past two days. Luckily, the doctors said he would be fine.

"I'm more worried about you," Chen said. "How are *you* doing?"

Zac shrugged. "I'll be fine. I guess it doesn't hurt to think like my dad in situations like this." He offered a fake smile. "That we're all just pawns of fate who have no control over our lives."

Emilee walked up and held Zac's hand. "You have control," she said. "We all do."

Zac shook his head. "I don't know. Maybe. So do you think it was fate that Rock was attacked like that? That everything that happened to us these past two weeks was all supposed to lead up to this?"

"We'll never know," Emilee said. "All that's clear is the future. Even Rock accepts that he can only keep looking ahead. He's going to make a full recovery, at least. And because of his injuries, doctors were able to analyze the proteins found in the venom. They think they may be able to use it to make some advances in medicine. He says he wishes he could be here."

"Thanks," Zac said.

"So where is Bryce right now?" Chen asked.

Zac started walking toward his car, and they followed. "He's in a hospital. A place where he can get counseling. When I took him there and left him, it was only one hour in the past, so it's not like he's in a different time period or anything."

"That was smart," Emilee said. "When I told your dad what was happening, he wanted to find a place for Bryce to get help. He said that he was going to talk to Bryce and take him there himself if he could, but it was too late by then."

Zac gave a small smile. "Even in his last moments, my dad didn't want me to give up on Bryce."

"They were pretty close," Emilee said. "Bryce saw your dad as a father figure because he never had one growing up. And he kind of became a rebellious son. He couldn't lash out at his real dad, so he targeted the person he was closest to. Someone he knew would still care about him no matter what he did."

TWENTY SEVEN

Bryce sat in his room, reading. It had been a month since he had been left at the counseling center. The staff was confused as to how he had gotten there, and they just assumed that he had checked himself in. At first, he denied it and fought against their efforts, but he knew that if he started talking about time travel and wormholes, he would be committed. He chose to cooperate.

He was starting to doze off when a voice woke him.

"Hi, Bryce."

He thought it was a counselor, but when he looked up, he was surprised to see Zac standing in his room.

"Zac?" he asked. He felt relief at the sight of him. But something was different. Zac was different.

"How are you?" Zac asked. His voice was deeper, older. He had a small beard now, stubble of facial hair covering his chin and face.

"What... what happened?" Bryce asked. "How'd you get in here? I didn't hear anyone let you in."

Zac moved closer. Bryce stepped back, afraid Zac would do something to harm him.

"Five years happened," Zac said. "For you, it's been... what? A month or two?"

Bryce nodded. "A little over a month. Yeah."

Zac looked away. "Bryce, for the past five years, I've lived with the burden of watching my mom die at my own hand. Of having my father die in my own arms."

Bryce hung his head in sadness. "I'm sorry," he said. "I know that doesn't mean anything, but if I could go back and stop myself from what I did, I would."

"That's not the point," Zac said. "I've had a lot of time to think. Five years gives a person a lot of time to reflect on what's important in life."

Bryce was on guard, not sure where Zac was going with this. "So why are you here?"

Zac turned, looking him square in the eyes. "You ruined just about every aspect of my life," he said. "I trusted you. You were supposed to help me, but instead, you made my life miserable."

Bryce was silent.

"I spent years fighting the thought of getting even with you, ways I could make you feel the way you made me feel." He sat down and softened his tone. "But after all that time, I realized that no matter what I did, it wouldn't bring my parents back. You already suffered through the loss of your mom. If I did something worse, it wouldn't make my life any better."

"Again, Zac, I'm sorry. The people here have helped me so much in this short time."

Zac held up his hand to stop Bryce. "Here's what I decided to do," Zac said. "When I went back to stop you, and I saw my mom again, I felt so good. It was like a second chance to see her again, even though it was short-lived. But those precious minutes were like another lifetime to me. I've thought about it, and I've realized that the only way I could truly heal would be to help you heal."

Bryce stared at him, curious. "What do you mean?"

"I'm going to give you a second chance, Bryce. I'm going to let you see her again."

"But I can't change anything."

"No," Zac said, "but we can at least look at that moment in the past and treasure it, holding it forever." He held out the Wand he had used. "I'm going to take you to let you see her. But it's just that; you are not supposed to interact with her or tell her who you are. Got it?"

Bryce smiled and nodded. "Seriously? After all I've done, you'd do this for me?"

"Yes," Zac said. "My dad's last request was that I don't give up on you. And if he cared that much about you, so should I."

Zac put his arm around Bryce's shoulder as if they were old friends and pressed the button on the Wand.

The street they arrived on was part of an older town. Bryce estimated it had to be about twenty years ago or so. The signs were different, and in the old downtown square, music played over the speakers.

"Where are we?" he asked. Zac led him across the town square and in front of a store with a "Now Hiring" sign. The store had a banner across the front window declaring that it was open for business; they hadn't even put up the name of the store yet.

"Come on," Zac said. "And remember what I told you." He pushed open the door, and the bell rang to indicate a customer was present.

Sweet smells of a bakery filled the air, and Bryce breathed them in deeply. "Can we stop to eat?" he asked. "This smells great, and I could go for something different."

"Sure," Zac said. He sat down at a table.

Bryce pulled up a chair and admired the old building. "So what are we doing here?" he asked. He looked at the glass case that displayed the freshly-cooked pastries. There were cupcakes with mounds of icing, donuts with pink frosting, cake donuts, donut holes... he wanted to sample every kind.

"You told me your mom used to go to a donut shop every day, right?"

"Yeah," Bryce said. "But I never knew where it was."

Zac smiled. "I did a little searching, and I believe that you're sitting in it."

Bryce froze. He spun around and looked at the door. "You mean... you mean my mom could walk through that door any minute?"

"Exactly," Zac said. "But we're only here so you can see her, not talk to her."

"I know, I know," he said, both excited and grateful. "I know the rules." It was like a completely different Bryce was sitting before him, one that was happier even than when Zac first met him. He tapped his feet and looked back and forth expectantly.

No one came. After half an hour, he started to give up hope.

"Maybe it's the wrong one," Zac said. "I'm sorry."

Bryce's shoulders sunk. "It's okay," he said. "I appreciate the fact that you at least came to me. I still can't believe that you'd do something nice for me."

Zac shrugged. "I've had five years to think about it. The 'me' running around in your present is still bitter, still angry at having to live with relatives." He pushed in his chair.

A sound from the back of the shop made them turn. A short man wearing a blue button-up shirt and black pants walked out.

"I'm so sorry," he said. "I didn't even hear you two come in. How long have you been waiting?"

"Oh, not long," Zac said. "We were just about to head out, though."

"Don't go," the manager said. "The person I hired told me today that he took another job, so right now it's just me. I've been trying to find someone who can help out, but I haven't found anyone. No chance either of you guys could give me a hand for an hour or so, could you?" He offered them a hopeful smile.

Bryce turned to Zac and shrugged. "I don't have any place to be," he said. "I've got all the time in the world, really."

Zac gave him a stern look, but then relented. "One hour," he said. "Then we really need to get going."

The manager beamed and led Bryce behind the counter, tossing him an apron. "All you need to do is chat up the customers and feed them," he said. "Make them feel at home so they come back. I'll go get you an apron. Be right back." He disappeared through the door into the kitchen.

The bell to the front door rang, and a young woman clothed in a red dress adorned with flowers walked in. Her stomach protruded slightly, bulging just above her waist.

"Hi, can I help you?" Bryce asked, then stopped when he looked up. A smile spread across his face, bigger than one Zac had ever seen, and his tone changed. "Um… how about a donut on the house this morning?"

"Really?" the woman asked. "That's sweet!"

"Well," Bryce said, "it looks like you're eating for two right now anyway. And you're our first customer of the day."

The woman continued smiling and stood next to the counter, her pregnant belly pressing against the glass.

"I'm Bryce," he said. He couldn't believe he was seeing her again. She looked so young and radiant. And she was here, standing right in front of him, talking to him again.

"Kathryn," she said. "Nice to meet you."

Bryce looked at Zac, who motioned for him to talk in private.

"Uh, would you excuse me?" he asked. "I need to talk with that gentleman for a moment, and then I'll be right with you."

"Sure," she said. Her smile was as beautiful as he remembered it.

Bryce hurried over to Zac. "It's her," he said. His eyes began filling with tears. "And I can't even go over and hug her."

"I know," Zac said, placing his hand on Bryce's shoulder.

"No," Bryce said, recoiling from Zac's touch. "Not now, please. Let me talk to her a little longer. I don't want to just see her and go back. I want to spend more time here."

"Bryce," Zac said, putting his hand back on his shoulder, "I don't think you see what's happening here."

"What do you mean?" Bryce asked.

Zac smiled. "I think you're going to be doing a lot of talking with her from now on."

Bryce stood there, unsure of what Zac was talking about. Finally, the realization hit him. "You mean..."

"Yeah," Zac said. "I think this is how you got your name."

Bryce's lip was quivering now. "You won't make me go back? I can stay here?"

"I think so," Zac said. "But you have to make a promise that you won't try to change anything. That you'll just live a normal life."

Bryce turned to look at his mother, who was examining all of the donuts under the glass. "Every day," he whispered.

"Every day," Zac said. "Just like you said."

"But why? Why are you letting me do this?"

"Because," Zac said, "I've come to see that my dad might have been right. Some things are meant to be." He slapped Bryce on the back. "Good luck," he said.

Zac watched as Bryce walked over to his mother again. The two of them talked, and he could see the love radiating between them. He was being given a second chance. Bryce said he was named after a man who cared about his mother, the man who made an impact on her heart and soul. The same man who would make her feel like the most important person in the world. Zac now knew why that was.

As Zac stepped out of the donut shop and onto the sidewalk, he turned and waved goodbye. Bryce and his mom waved back, and Zac knew that Bryce was at home now, here in this time and place. This is where Bryce would spend the rest of his days, where he was always meant to. Some things can never be changed.

ACKNOWLEDGEMENTS

First, I must thank my wife Jo Ann for all of her support. From the inception of the idea to the revision stage, she has been a tireless cheerleader of my work, encouraging me to complete the story even when it became difficult. Writing is no easy task, but she makes it easier.

I also need to thank Bethany and Owen, who have had to endure their dad going out periodically to focus on writing.

Thanks also goes to Jim Sutton, whose enthusiasm for time travel stories helped me avoid inconsistencies in the timeline.

My parents have always encouraged my writing from a young age, from printing up my old newsletters to buying me my first typewriter.

Finally, a huge thank you goes to my students, the beta readers who gave honest feedback on the drafts to let me know what worked and what didn't. They helped me shape the story into what it is today.

ABOUT THE AUTHOR

Although not a superhero, C. David Milles does have a dual identity. He is a middle school teacher by day and a writer by night. He enjoys exploring the building blocks of stories, especially through the lens of the Hero's Journey.

He loves all things geeky: superheroes, video games, reading, and writing. His favorites include television shows like *Lost*, *Fringe*, and *Doctor Who*, and movies like *Jurassic Park*, *Indiana Jones*, *Lord of the Rings,* and *Back to the Future*.

He is married and has two children.

You can follow him on his writing blog, *Attacking Ideas 101*.

http://cdavidmilles.blogspot.com